Outlaw Brand

Outlaw Brand

Todhunter Ballard

THORNDIKE
CHIVERS

This Large Print edition is published by Thorndike Press®, Waterville, Maine USA and by BBC Audiobooks, Ltd, Bath, England.

Published in 2005 in the U.S. by arrangement with Golden West Literary Agency.

Published in 2005 in the U.K. by arrangement with Golden West Literary Agency.

U.S. Hardcover 0-7862-7592-8 (Western)
U.K. Hardcover 1-4056-3386-7 (Chivers Large Print)
U.K. Softcover 1-4056-3387-5 (Camden Large Print)

A shorter version of this novel appeared serially in *Ranch Romances* under the title "Railroad Doctor."

The text of this Large Print edition is unabridged.
Other aspects of the book may vary from the original edition.

Set in 16 pt. Plantin by Al Chase.

Printed in the United States on permanent paper.

British Library Cataloguing-in-Publication Data available

Library of Congress Cataloging-in-Publication Data

Bonner, Parker, 1903–
    Outlaw brand / by Todhunter Ballard writing as Parker Bonner.
        p. cm. — (Thorndike Press large print Westerns)
    ISBN 0-7862-7592-8 (lg. print : hc : alk. paper)
    1. Ex-convicts — Fiction. 2. Judicial error — Fiction.
3. Train robberies — Fiction. 4. Large type books.
I. Title. II. Thorndike Press large print Western series.
PS3503.A5575O94 2005
813'.6—dc22   2005003795

Outlaw Brand

chapter 1

Andy Lawrence perched himself comfortably on the top of the empty baggage truck to watch the arrival of the through sleeper from the East.

It was a daily ritual for him, since like most of the boys in Soda Springs he fully intended to become a railroad man.

Originally he had planned to be an engineer. The men who ran the locomotive equipment were considered the princes of the road, but Andy had already figured out that while the engine man might be the more colorful, the dispatcher exercised the real power, and with this in mind he had gone out of his way to make friends with Boone Grantline.

The dispatcher lived at the hotel which was run by Andy's mother, and he had readily agreed to teach Andy the code and how to use the key. The offer had come only that morning, and Andy was thinking about it as the heavy train rolled in and the passengers hurried down the steps and dashed toward the lunchroom.

Andy had a true desert boy's contempt for these Eastern travelers with their white, unburned skins and their odd uncomfortable clothes, and he paid little attention until the tall man came up to him.

"Hi, son." The voice was friendly. "Don't they run the hack any more?"

Andy came out of his daydream, in which he had pictured himself as running the whole division, and looked at the newcomer. He decided the man was a drummer.

"You looking for a hotel?"

The man nodded, and the boy's interest came to life. "You've got three choices," he said. "The Railroad Hotel is noisy. The Palmer House is quieter, but they rob you. Now, if you want a quiet place with good food and clean beds, why, my mother runs the Apache."

The man grinned. "I guess the Apache sounds about right."

Andy slid from his perch. "You won't be sorry. I'm Andy Lawrence."

The man showed surprise. "You Dave Lawrence's boy? How is Dave?"

"He's dead," Andy said, and the warmth had gone from his voice.

"Dead?" All expression faded from the man's face, leaving it cold, a little bleak.

"Dead. But he wasn't old —"

"He was murdered, a year ago Christmas morning."

The man stared down at the small face, as taut and resolute as his own. "Dave murdered. But who —"

"If I knew I'd shoot them." Andy was trying to mask his grief by sullenness as he stooped to pick up the man's bags. "And when we get to the hotel, don't tell Ma I said anything. I'm not supposed to talk about it."

The man took the heavy bags from the boy's hands. "Why not, Andy?"

Andy shrugged. "Ma says that it won't bring Pa back, and they never found out who shot him, and they never will, and she just doesn't want it to make me bitter."

The man's voice was soft. "I knew your father very well, Andy. In fact I came back here, partly to prove that he hadn't made a mistake in giving me his help. I'm Hippocrates West."

Andy, who had been leading the way across the station yard, turned to stare at him. He had heard the name all his life. The town still gossiped about West, about the nameless boy who had been raised by the Bentons in the northern breaks, who had helped the older Benton boys hold up a train and been knocked from his saddle by a posse bullet.

Yes, Andy knew the full story: how the boy had been brought to town more dead than alive and how he had nearly been sent to the Territorial Prison, along with Prince and Duke Benton.

He would have gone to prison if it had not been for Andy's father and for Doc Condon, who had taken the youthful outlaw into his own home.

Condon had taken him in and given him a name. He had called him Hippocrates West, and the name had amused the town. But it had not amused Andy's father, who had snorted:

"Hippocrates West! Hippocrates, my foot. I don't care if this Hippocrates did start the medical business. It's a hell of a name to mark a kid with. Why couldn't Condon have called him Bill, or Pete or Frank? It will mark him, and no one will ever forget who he was or that he helped hold up that train."

Andy hadn't forgotten, although it was more than six years since West had run away. There had been some loose talk about trailing him then, about bringing him back and sending him to the prison, but nothing had ever come of it.

And now West was back, and Andy was as excited at meeting him as if he had seen Billy the Kid or one of the Earps.

He stuttered as he said, "Doc Condon will sure be surprised to see you."

West looked down at him. "How is Doc?"

"Mean as ever. Ma says he'll never change, and he'll never die. He keeps himself pickled all the time." They crossed the broad street and came into the narrow lobby of the Apache Hotel, Andy racing ahead to shout:

"Ma! Hey, Ma! Guess who's here!"

Mary Lawrence was small and quick and bird-like, and her face in spite of its crown of white hair was still young looking. She came from the dining room, wiping her hands on her apron, saying in a reproving voice, "Don't shout. What will the gentleman think?"

"He's not a gentleman," Andy said. "He's Hippocrates West."

Mary Lawrence stopped. Then her face warmed and she came forward to stand on tip-toe and peck a kiss against West's cheek. For an instant the action startled him. Then he dropped his bags, picked her up in his powerful arms and swung her around, her feet well clear of the floor.

"That's the finest homecoming a man

ever had." He kissed her then, full on the lips.

Mary Lawrence was flustered. "Hy West, you put me down. I'm old enough to be your mother."

"But too pretty," he said. The laughter died from his eyes. He set her gently on her feet and said, softly, "I wish you were, ma'am. I do for a fact. Andy doesn't know how lucky he is."

chapter 2

Andy Lawrence retreated to the kitchen as his mother showed West up to his room. Andy was anxious to spread the news of West's sudden return, but his eagerness was tempered by his appetite and he was helping himself to a slice of bread and jam when Belle Callahan came from the laundry and caught him.

She was a large girl and her face was slightly broad and her features had the irregularity which so often marks the Irish; but her mouth was wide and generous, her gray-blue eyes kind and friendly and understanding.

"Andy!" She caught him by the back of his jacket. "You know you aren't allowed to piece between meals."

He struggled to keep the bread out of her reach. "I know something you don't know. Hy West just came back, and old Doc Condon don't even know he's home."

She let go her grip in surprise. "Hy West?"

"That's right."

13

She said in a strange voice, "What did the fool come back here for?"

Andy retreated to a corner, but he was puzzled. To him, Soda Springs was the greatest town on earth. "Why shouldn't he come back?"

"Why should he? They treated him like a dog, and the kids at school made fun of him until he wore his guns one day. They stopped mighty quick, believe me."

Andy was staring at her. "You knew him? You knew the Orphan Kid?"

"I went to school with him."

"Gee, you're old."

She laughed at him then. She had to. She was twenty-two. Then she turned and the laughter died, for West was standing in the dining room doorway.

He came forward, and neither spoke for a moment. Then he said, softly, "Hi, Belle."

"Hello," she said, her eyes studying him, noting the changes that six years had wrought. "I never expected to see you here again."

"Why not?" he said. "I told you I was going away and get to be a doctor, and then come back and show them all."

She walked over to lean one hand against the table. "And are you a doctor, Hy?"

He nodded, his tight lips smiling a little.

"Even have a paper to prove it."

"But why did you come back?"

"Why not? I said I would."

This stopped her for a moment. There was a hard core in this man which had always frightened her a little, a hard purpose which carried him forward against all and any odds.

She said, slowly, "You'll get no practice here. It surely would have been easier to stay in the East."

He considered in silence. She had been his only friend in school, the only one of sixty children who had not looked on him as a kind of freak, and he had been bitter and lonely, not allowed to return to the Benton ranch by the court which had paroled him in Doctor Condon's care.

Belle had been something of an outcast herself. Her father had been a sergeant in the cavalry, stationed at the nearby fort, her mother a laundress for the officers, and the town children had considered that she was not one of them.

On this their friendship had been based, and it was to her that he had bragged that he would run away and be a doctor. She had not believed him. She had jeered at him until he struck her. Then they had fought, for in the hard world in which Belle had

15

been raised you asked no quarter simply because you happened to be a girl.

The town marshal had pulled them apart. The town marshal had locked him up, claiming that he was a danger to everyone in Soda Springs. And Callahan had come down and made the marshal turn the boy loose.

Callahan was no longer in the army. He had bought himself out and started a saloon, and was already becoming something of a power in the politics of the town. Callahan had gotten the boy free and walked down the street with him.

"It was my girl made me come," Callahan said. "She claims the fight was her fault. She says you're planning to run away."

West's cheek was puffed where Belle's hard little fist had caught him squarely. He did not answer. He did not trust Callahan. He did not trust anyone. He was bitter, and hurt, and savage as a cornered bear.

Callahan looked at him shrewdly. "I ran away," he said. "Nearly forty years ago. I met the Squire as I was leaving, and somehow he guessed and he gave me a shilling. A man should not be without money. I'm doing the same thing for you." He reached out and put a twenty dollar gold piece into West's palm.

The boy's first impulse was to run after the Irishman and throw the money in his face, but he did not. He left Soda Springs that night and now he was back.

He told her this, and said, "The first thing I want to do is to give your father back his money, to prove to him that it was not wasted."

"So that's what brought you back?"

His jaw set. "Look, Belle, you know what I took from this town, better than anyone else. It would have been simple to stay in the East, but all my life I'd have been haunted by the knowledge that I'd run away, that I was afraid to come back."

"But you'll starve," she said. "You can't expect the people here to accept an outlaw kid as a doctor."

He grinned then. "If that is all that worries you, forget it. I knew what the town's reaction would be. I have no plans to go into general practice. I'm the new assistant at the Railroad Hospital."

She was startled. "Gruber's assistant?"

"I guess that's his name."

"Oh." She could think of nothing more to say.

It was his turn to ask a question. "What are you doing here?"

She told him levelly, "I'm the hired girl."

He was surprised. Even before he had left Soda Springs Callahan's saloon was prospering and he said in some embarrassment, "Your father. I thought —"

"That I would not have to work?" She did not pretend to misunderstand. "I don't — not if I were willing to live on what the saloon makes — but I don't like that kind of money. I don't hold with liquor, any more than my mother did. She left Callahan when he started the place, and I'd be a hypocrite if I were willing to live on money that was made in a way I don't approve of."

He stared at her, and she smiled. "Don't worry about me. Mary Lawrence, bless her, is wonderful to work for." She glanced at the watch pinned to the front of her shirtwaist. "Which reminds me. It's time to start supper. We can talk later."

West turned away slowly, knowing he had been dismissed. For six years he had pictured his return, and for some reason which he did not clearly understand, he felt let down.

He left the kitchen, crossed the lobby and stepped out into the street. As soon as he left the shelter of the wooden gallery the afternoon sun beat down upon him with fierce intensity. Under the whitish glare the town still dozed in its late siesta. Even the shrill whistles of the slowly moving switch engines in the big yards had taken on a sleepy note.

Soda Springs was a railroad town, a division point, with all the faults and vices and dirtiness which went with such a place. It was not different from a hundred other such towns, but its setting was different in that it perched uneasily on the desert which stretched out to the south and east like the irregular folds of a carelessly spread blanket.

Only to the north and west was there a hint of beauty, for here in the near distance rose the timbered peaks of the higher watered country, dark mountains edging a broken land which was so rough that men seldom rode through it.

Along the edges of this plateau-like formation were the tumbled canyons which corkscrewed their water courses into the flat lands below. Small ranchers had built their homesteads in these canyons, battling the thin feed, the rocky soil and the howling winters.

Above them were a few mines, their starving owners following the faulted veins which laced their circuitous way through the volcanic torture of the county rock.

It was a poor country, a troubled country, a place which had known violence and strife long before the railroad punched through its right-of-way, and built the town by establishing its shops, its division point and its hotel.

But the coming of the railroad had not changed the basic pattern of local life. The railroad workers battled the ranchers and the miners. The outlaws lurking in the rough country swept down occasionally, raiding the more prosperous ranches and the railroad alike, ignoring the fact that the Territorial Prison reared its grim walls less than thirty miles to the west.

And to highlight the uncertainty the Indians were continually restless on their unproductive reservations, kept in check by a nervous and understaffed army.

This was the land in which West had been raised, and this was the land to which he had returned, feeling as much a stranger as if he had never lived here.

It was difficult for him to associate himself with the reckless boy who had ridden with the Bentons, who had sneered at the court after the train robbery, and who had run away.

He glanced along the street, seeing no activity in the grip of the afternoon heat. A dozen horses, apparently forgotten by their owners, stood hip-shot at the rails, their heads bowed, the only sign of life the constant switching of their tails to drive away the persistently buzzing flies.

West's movements were unhurried and he breathed the dusty air sparingly, already feeling the parched dryness which seemed to sear his lungs. He was glad to turn out of the glare into the comparative coolness of Callahan's saloon.

The room into which he came was semi-dark and he paused an instant to allow his contracted pupils to accustom themselves to the gloom.

It was an old trick, born of those early years when each room he entered might hold an enemy and where sun-blindness might bring a quick, sharp, jarring death.

He no longer felt that he was hunted, or that every man's hand was against him, but his pause was an instinct of those other days when he had ridden the outlaw trail.

As soon as his vision sharpened he saw that the big room was hardly changed. It seemed a little dirtier, its bar a little more scuffed, its swinging lamps a little more dented. But the same smell still lingered, a mingling of old dust, and tobacco smoke, and spilled beer and human sweat.

Callahan was behind the bar, his bulging middle under its dirty apron giving the lie to the fact that only ten years before he had been the hardest riding sergeant in the old Third Cavalry.

He was a moose of a man, his dark hair cut so short that the scars which marred his round skull showed plainly in remembrance of a thousand fights. An explosive man, handsome in his own way, his features reminding West of Belle Callahan.

Callahan had been watching the game at one of the rear poker tables when West entered. Standing behind the bar, his big hands resting on the dark surface, he was tall enough to see over the heads of the small crowd.

He turned his head and, failing to recognize the newcomer, turned back to watch the play of the cards. West walked back along the bar toward him, drew a gold twenty dollar piece from his pocket and laid it before the saloon man.

"I'm returning the loan with thanks."

Callahan looked at the gold piece, then lifted his eyes to the younger man's face. "Well, I'll be damned." His voice had an explosive quality which filled the big room and turned every head at the card table toward them. "You're the kid that ran away to be a doctor." He extended a thick palm. "When did you get back?"

West shook hands. "At noon."

"How'd you make out, getting to be a doctor?"

"I made out. I am one."

"The saints preserve us. Belle said you would but I didn't believe it." He stared at the gold piece, frowning. "That wasn't a loan. A man gave me a shilling once. I passed it on to you. You pass it to someone else for luck."

West hesitated for the barest instant, then picked up the coin with a nod and dropped it into his vest pocket. In place of the gold he drew out a handful of change. "I'll buy a drink for the house."

He turned to glance at the men around the poker table. None of them nodded in greeting. None of them seemed to know who he was; none but an untidy man who sat at an otherwise empty table to the left of the card game. He had been taking no part in the play, but he had watched the fall of each card with the same concentrated attention that he might have used if the chips in the center of the table had all been his.

He was Doctor Condon, and West looked at him with real attention. The old Doc had saved his life by digging a bullet out of him, and then taken him into his home rather than let the court send a boy to prison.

But in some ways living with Condon had

23

been worse than prison. He had never understood the man. Sometimes, when deep in drink, Condon would discuss medicine. He had a real love for his profession, although he would scoff at it when he was sober. At other times he would rail at West, calling him ignorant and stupid and dumb, a brush jumper without education.

It was these attacks which had decided West that at all costs he would become a doctor. He had never told Condon of his ambition. He had told no one but Belle, and she had jeered, and they had fought, and he had run away.

Beside Condon lay a dirty, white dog with a long-nosed head and yellow coyote eyes. West did not need to be told that it was a mean dog, a vicious dog. He knew the strain, guessing that it was a grandson or great-grandson of the bitch which had nipped at his legs when he lived with Condon.

The dog was ugly, but no uglier than its master. Condon's head was bald, save for a fringe of mouse-colored hair around the edge. His eyes were blood-shot and he was untidy. He looked older than he was because of personal sloppiness.

He sat at the table, not moving beyond a fluttery gesture of his fingers on the dog's neck, showing no expression as he stared at West.

But West knew Condon was surprised. It was very evident that the news of his return had not yet reached this saloon. Then Condon said, "So you're a doctor?" Apparently he had heard what West had said to Callahan.

"I never expected to live to drink to your being a doctor." He watched as Callahan set the filled glass at his elbow, then lifted it slowly.

"It's a strange world, full of strange turnings." He downed the drink at a gulp, set the glass on the table and added in his rumbling voice, "So you've come back. You're going to repay my care by taking my practice away from me?"

West shook his head. He had expected no greeting from Condon save sarcasm and jeers; that was the way the older doctor greeted the whole world. But it had not occurred to him that Condon would think that he had returned to rob the older man of his practice.

"I'm not going into private practice," he said. "I'm here to work at the Railroad Hospital."

For the first time a gleam of real interest showed in Condon's yellowish eyes. "Don't

25

tell me the railroad finally got some sense and fired Gruber?"

"I'm to be his assistant."

Condon started to laugh then, the sound appearing to originate far down in his big belly. The laughter rose in a cascade of noise which seemed to fill the long, smoky room.

"Well I'll be damned," he said when he had recovered enough breath to speak. "This is the end. That snot-nosed bastard hasn't enough to do to keep one man busy so they send him an assistant. No wonder they say the whole road is going broke. It's a good thing they don't have a hospital in every town. There wouldn't be enough doctors in the world to keep them going."

The men at the near table laughed. Callahan didn't. West sensed that Callahan was watching him, and he knew that in the saloon man's eyes he was undergoing his first test.

If he allowed Condon to make a fool of him the story would be told all over town by evening. Each action he took would be watched, for he was marked. He had known this before he returned and he knew that in this country a man was judged by his ability to handle himself in any situation.

Inside he felt grim, but he managed a

laugh, knowing that it was not too good an effort, knowing that it had a forced sound.

But when he spoke his tone was easy. "Sounds like I won't be over-worked," he said. "Sounds like I'll have plenty of time to take care of the mistakes you been making around here for years, Doc."

The laughter in the room grew, and for the moment he had turned it against Condon. He had no intention of losing his advantage. He nodded to Callahan, said to Condon, "See you later," and moved easily down the room toward the door. Behind him the laughter had died. Behind him was no sound but the growling of the white dog.

On the street Hy West felt better. Condon was known as the sharpest wit in town. To turn the laugh on him was an achievement. He crossed to the hotel, entered it and crossed the lobby.

He had reached the bottom of the stairs and was just starting upward toward the room when he heard the noise from the kitchen: a man swearing sharply, and Belle Callahan's muffled answer.

He moved quickly through the dining room to the kitchen door. He pushed it open and found Belle struggling in a man's arms. The man's back was toward West, and he did not know that the doctor was in the room until West seized his shoulders, jerking him free of the girl.

West held him for an instant, then spun him across the room. He stumbled over the ironing board which had been standing beside the table and went crashing into the big range, his hands outstretched in an effort to break his fall. They came down flat on the smoking top.

He jerked erect with a high shout of pain, and pivoted to meet the newcomer. As he turned, West realized that it was Bo Benton, the youngest of the family.

For an instant Benton was motionless, surprised at seeing West. Then he swore hoarsely. "The Kid!"

West waited, his powerful body a little crouched. Of all the Bentons he had liked Bo the least. Bo was a braggart, Bo had picked on him when he was a child because West had been smaller. Bo had stolen his things, and made him do work which was rightfully Bo's.

He felt a surge of anger rise through him, but he curbed it, saying in a flat voice, "Get out of here, Bo."

The youngest Benton showed his teeth in a wicked smile. Like all of his breed he would fight at any time, merely for the love of fighting, and he had always disliked the younger man. He had not understood this dislike himself, nor realized that it stemmed from his inner knowledge that West was smarter than he, and that he was actually jealous of the orphan.

He had had several drinks, priming himself to enter the hotel kitchen, and the drinks inflamed him now.

Without answering he charged, throwing a wicked left into West's stomach which doubled the doctor over. As West bent forward, Bo grabbed his shoulders, holding him thus for an instant as he brought up his knee sharply, trying for West's jaw.

But he missed, for although his first blow had driven most of the air from the doctor's body, West still had enough sense left to catch the lifting leg and throw himself backward, heaving upward as he did so, thus dumping Bo onto his back on the scrubbed floor.

He knew from long experience that no Benton would ever stop a fight as long as he could move. He dived onto the fallen man, using his weight and the strength of his arms in an effort to smother him.

There was no science. They fought as they had fought always, like two young animals. But they were both much bigger now, much heavier, and their fists did far more damage.

The advantage lay with Benton. He was heavier, the veteran of a hundred barroom fights, and his muscles were the harder since West had done little physical work during the last six years.

But a determination rode West. There was something in him which drove him forward, even when it seemed that he was beaten. They broke finally, rolling clear and struggling to their feet to stand toe to toe, slugging until Benton was forced to clinch.

Then they went down again, locked in each other's arms. This time Benton landed on top.

West lay for an instant, gasping for breath. Then he twisted, arched, and managed to throw Benton from him. Benton rolled over and over until he was near the stove. He came to his knees, and made no effort to rise farther. Instead his hand dropped to the heavy gun in his belt and dragged it clear of the holster.

He raised it, using the last of his faltering strength and centered the heavy barrel on West's chest, saying in a ragged voice, "I'm going to kill you, Kid."

West stood beside the center table. He had used it to drag himself to his feet. He swayed, his eyes bloodshot. He was not in much better shape than Benton, but in his own heart he knew that he had won. The very fact that Bo Benton had been forced to pull his gun proved he admitted West was the better man.

Still, the knowledge would be of little good to one who was dead, and he never thought for an instant that Bo would hesitate to shoot.

He was too far away to dive for the gun. There was no possible weapon on the table, not even a bread knife.

He stood staring at Benton, watching for the man's anger to tighten on the trigger. Belle Callahan was watching also. Belle had been raised in a hard school, and she looked around quickly for a weapon. The first thing she saw was a flatiron, smoking on the heated stove. Without hesitation she seized a potholder and then snatched up the iron. Leaning across one corner of the stove, she pressed the iron squarely between Bo Benton's shoulder blades.

The gun in Bo's hand exploded as he jumped straight into the air, the bullet digging into the floor at West's feet. Then Bo fell, squirming onto his back as if by so doing he could stop the burning sensation between his shoulders.

West jumped, even as the girl swung up the iron, and grabbed the gun which had dropped from Bo's hand. He watched Bo Benton try to dance upon his back, and for the life of him he could not help laughing.

Bo gave up trying to rub out the burn against the floorboards. He struggled to his knees, glaring upward at the man who now held his gun.

"I'll kill you for this, Kid."

"Get out."

Benton rose slowly. "I'll kill you."

West didn't bother to answer. He squeezed the heavy gun's trigger. The noise of the explosion filled the kitchen, and a neat hole appeared in the scrubbed boards between Benton's booted feet.

Bo stared at the hole as if he did not believe his eyes. West fired again. This time the bullet knocked the heel off of Bo's right boot.

Benton had had enough. He turned and leaped out through the kitchen door to the alley beyond. He had never before run from any man, but he ran now.

West made no move to follow. Belle Callahan was suddenly laughing as if she could not stop. Andy came racing in from the main room, attracted by the shots, just as Hy West thrust the big gun into the waistband of his trousers.

"What happened? Who'd you kill?"

Belle Callahan told him. The story was too good to keep. She picked up the iron she had dropped and returned it to the stove. Andy was gazing at West with big eyes. He said, slowly,

"I wouldn't want the Bentons after me. I sure wouldn't. That Bo is bad."

West didn't answer. He knew that Andy spoke the truth.

chapter 3

Andy Lawrence was having a wonderful time. He had traveled from one end of Railroad Avenue to the other, telling the story of Hy West's homecoming and of Bo Benton's fight and branding. It was not often that the town heard such a funny story, especially about the Bentons, and it spread like wildfire.

Andy loved to talk, and he loved to be the center of attention, but suddenly he lost interest in furthering the spreading of news. His quick eye had seen two riders turn in to the foot of the street, and he identified them almost at once as Bentons.

He stopped before a grocery store and, standing under the shelter of its gallery, partly hidden by a barrel of potatoes, he watched them come toward him.

The Bentons usually left the town pretty much alone, but once or twice each month they rode in, generally quarrelsome, especially after they had had a few drinks, and they seldom left without trouble of some kind.

Andy watched them, then turned to see

Bruce Gimble coming toward him from the opposite direction. Gimble habitually rode the streets at this hour of the evening, looking big and important behind the glitter of his marshal's star.

Andy did not like Gimble. With the ability of the adolescent to ferret out the weakness of adults he had long ago decided that Bruce Gimble, behind all his bluster, was a coward. He and his friend Sam Dillon had waited for months, hoping that Gimble and the Bentons would meet head-on sometime when the outlaws were feeling mean.

Like most of the boys in Soda Springs, Andy was both a little afraid and also a little proud of the Bentons. He marveled at the way they came and went, careless of the fact that half the people in the Territory hated them for their arrogance, their bullying ways, and the occasions when they shot up the town for pure meanness.

He looked again at them and then back at Gimble. A sneer grew on his young lips, for the marshal had sighted the oncoming riders and swung south onto Fremont, obviously to avoid meeting them.

It was not a new thing for Gimble to remain practically invisible when the outlaws were in town. He was only following his cautious custom, so that he would not be called upon to enforce the local ordinance which forbade the wearing of guns within the town limits.

Andy watched the Bentons pass. There were only two of them and they seemed very peaceful, so Andy decided that there would be no excitement from them, at least until later.

Disappointed, he moved on up Wichita Avenue to the Dillon house, but Sam was not at home. Andy turned back aimlessly, feeling lonely. He drifted across Railroad Avenue to the station platform just as the night limited rolled in from the East.

He noticed the girl first because she was pretty, small, and blonde, and very striking in her city clothes. The rest of the passengers did not bring luggage as they stepped down and headed for the lunchroom, but a trainman followed her down the steps carrying her bags. He set them on the platform, and she looked around as if for help.

Andy was at her side in a moment, sensing a chance for profit. "Help you, ma'am?"

She turned to smile at him. "Why, perhaps you can. I'm looking for a Doctor West. He used to live here and he just came home recently."

Andy's interest jumped. "Of course I know him. He's staying at our hotel." He stooped and picked up her bag, finding it surprisingly light. "Is he a friend of yours?"

He was already piloting her through the crowd, and her laugh made him turn. "I guess you'd call him a friend," she said. "At least I came out here to marry him."

Andy had absorbed more surprises that day than he usually did in a month. He recovered enough to ask, "What's your name?"

"Laura Hall."

"You know Hy at Chicago?"

"I was a nurse there. Do you think Hy will be at the hotel now?"

The boy nodded. "He's lying down in his room."

Laura Hall was surprised. West was not the kind to go to bed early. "Is he sick?"

This was the opening Andy had been playing for. "Well, I wouldn't say that he was exactly sick. He had a fight with Bo Benton, and he's a mite battered up."

"Fight?" Laura Hall stopped. In the years she had known West he had never fought anyone. "What in the world was he fighting about?"

"Well, Bo tried to kiss our hired girl, and Doc stopped him and they fought, and then Bo pulled his gun, and Belle, that's the hired girl, she branded him with a hot iron, and Doc grabbed Bo's gun and shot his heel off."

Laura was staring at him. "You aren't making this up?"

Andy was indignant. "You can ask Hy. That's just the way it happened, so help me."

Laura Hall bit her lip. The boy's words, more than the people they passed as they moved up Railroad Avenue, made her realize what a different world this was from the one she knew. The sun had dropped behind the western mountains, but there was still enough light for her to see the people on the street: shirt-sleeved men, their wide-brimmed hats pushed back from sunburned faces, ten men for every woman.

She wondered again if she had not made a mistake in coming here. In the lobby, facing Mary Lawrence as she wrote her name in the smudged register, her doubt grew. She must see West at once.

Mary Lawrence was having one of her spells, and Andy showed the new guest to her room, lit the lamp and made certain the pitcher on the washstand contained water.

She opened her purse and put a silver dollar into his small hand. Andy stared at it as if he had never seen a dollar before. Certainly no one at the hotel had ever given him one. The usual reward for carrying their bags was a dime, or a quarter at most.

"That — that's too much."

She smiled. Laura Hall had used the same smile on older men with good results and it captivated Andy. "Which is Doctor West's room?"

Andy hesitated. He was old enough to know why his mother had such a strict rule about women in men's rooms, but with this girl he thought that it was different. Certainly she looked like a lady, not like Straight-Edge Ella's girls.

Andy knew all about the big house on the side street. He had run errands for them more than once. There were few things about Soda Springs and its citizens which Andy and Sam Dillon did not know.

He said, slowly, "You're not supposed to go to a man's room unless you're married to him."

She smiled again. "But Hy and I are going to be married."

Andy was still a little dubious, but he felt that there was small chance that his mother would find out, and Laura had given him the dollar. In the end he led her along the hall toward West's room.

Hy West had been lying in the warm darkness. He was fully dressed and he had no intention of going to bed, but his face was marked by Bo Benton's fists. He knew the story was probably all over town, and he wondered if it would be wise for him to leave the hotel on this night.

He heard their steps, and the knock on his door, and he said, "Come in," automatically.

The door opened. He saw Laura Hall standing in the oblong of light. "Laura!" He came off the bed at once, fumbling for a friction match, lighting the lamp. "Laura, where did you come from?"

Andy was an interested spectator, standing in the doorway as the girl entered the lighted room. West saw him and said, "Thanks for bringing her up, Andy." He walked over and shut the door. He stood there for a moment, listening. There was no sound of footsteps from the hall. He reopened the door.

"That's all, Andy."

The boy turned reluctantly and moved toward the head of the stairs. West waited until he started down, then closed the door again and turned back to the girl. He looked at her for a long moment in silence.

"I thought we said good-bye."

Tears were close behind her eyes, and she came forward uncertainly. "You asked me

40

to come out here with you. I said I wouldn't, and then, when I realized you were gone, I couldn't bear being alone. I got the next train."

Still he made no move to touch her. It was as if he had turned to stone. She hesitated for an instant, then stepped against him, her young body alive beneath the tightness of her dress, pressing against him, warming him, turning him alive.

He crushed her to him. She pushed him away, laughing up into his face. "You do still want me?"

He kissed her. All the loneliness which he had known through the years was welling up within him. That's what Laura had meant to him, a cure for loneliness. He really knew very little about her, for she talked only sketchily about herself. He knew that she was Polish with a name which was not Hall; that her father had been a stockyard worker with seven children; that she had run away from home at fourteen and managed to take nurses' training at a time when there were still few women in the profession.

She had not told him why she left home, how one of her father's drunken friends had taken her to bed with him. These things she had kept to herself.

Nor was she in love with West. She too

had been lonely, and they had drifted together, two strangers in a large city. At least, she realized, he was honest, and he had ability. He would go far once he was out of school, and she had attached herself to him, planning to marry him, hunting the security of being a successful doctor's wife.

Their affair had run through his school years, and it had come as a distinct shock to her when, after his graduation, West turned down a resident's job to accept a position in a railroad hospital in a remote Western town.

She had railed at him then. She had told him that he was crazy, that she did not mean to bury herself in any sagebrush village. But as soon as he was gone, she realized that without him she had no future. All the fine plans she had made collapsed, and never being one to hesitate when her comfort was involved, she had caught the next train for Soda Springs.

Now, standing in the bare hotel room, she was certain that she had again made a mistake. She needed the comfort of West's arms about her to steady her, to reassure her.

She said in a choked voice, "Why did you ever come back here?"

His voice was low, even. "I had to show them."

She pushed back so that she could see his face. "Had to show who? Had to show them what?"

He hesitated. "Look, Laura. I never talked much about myself at the hospital, about who I am or where I came from."

She realized that this was so, but she had never given it much thought. She had not talked much about her own early years, either.

"What difference does it make?"

He shrugged. "It made a difference to me. I was raised by a family named Benton. I never had a name. Sometimes they called me the orphan, sometimes the Orphan Kid."

She was staring at him, feeling the bitterness in his level tone.

"They were outlaws. I don't mean they were in hiding all the time. A lot of the outlaws in this country have their own places, and as long as they don't pull anything too raw the authorities leave them alone."

She didn't understand. It showed in her face.

"That's because there isn't much law out here, and the country is big, and pretty empty. The Bentons stole a few cattle and held up a stage now and then. But no one could prove it, and all of them were dangerous. And then we held up a train."

She drew her breath sharply. "You held up a train?"

"Well, I stayed with the horses. I was only fourteen. Anyhow, we got away with the express box, and started for the hills. A posse trailed us and cornered us up in the peaks, and I got a bullet in the shoulder." He stripped off his coat, and then his shirt to show her the white, diamond-like scar.

She had seen it before, but she had never questioned him. He went on, his voice still showing no emotion. "They caught us, Duke and Prince Benton and me. They had a trial and they sent Duke and Prince to prison for twenty years. But the sheriff told the judge I was too young, and a doctor named Condon offered to take me into his home and raise me. The court paroled me in his charge."

She said faintly, "That's where you got the idea of being a doctor?"

He nodded. "Condon was drunk half the time, and he treated me the way he treated a couple of mean dogs he had. He used to tell me I was too stupid to be a doctor, too stupid to be anything. I had a bad time. The kids at school called me an outlaw. The town felt I should have gone to prison. There was only one person who was halfway

44

decent to me, a girl, and I told her that I meant to be a doctor.

"Then she jeered at me. That was more than I could stand. We had a fight and the town marshal locked me up, and there was talk of them revoking my parole and sending me to prison. The girl's father came and got me out. He gave me twenty dollars and I ran away."

She was staring at him. "And after all that trouble you were fool enough to come back here?"

He said grimly, "I had to come back. I had to show this town and Condon that they were wrong about me, that I did have brains enough to become a doctor. I had to show the girl's father and the girl that I wasn't fooling, that I really meant to make something of myself."

Laura had a sudden thought. "That boy said you had a fight this afternoon, over some girl. Was that the same girl?"

He nodded.

She said, "Are you in love with her, Hy?"

He was startled. "In love with her? Of course not. I'm in love with you."

Laura had her own ideas about that. She had never been one to kid herself, and she was not kidding herself now. She knew that she had played upon West's loneliness, that

45

she had purposely excited him and taken him to bed with her. She knew, or thought she knew, that she could still hold him, but she resolved to be careful. Either he was in love with this other girl and did not know it, or he really had hated the town so strongly that he needed to come back to get even. And Laura believed that love was a much stronger emotion than hate. Certainly it was emotion of some kind which had brought West back. Reason hadn't. Reason would have kept him in Chicago where his future was assured.

chapter 4

Andy went unwillingly down the stairs. He was burning with curiosity and he resented the fact that West had sent him away. He turned through the dining room into the kitchen in search of his delayed supper, and Belle Callahan had to break off her ironing to feed him.

"One of these days when you don't show up at meal time you can go hungry."

The boy was not perturbed. He had heard the threat many times before. "How's Ma?"

"Not good. She's lying down in the back parlor. I don't like these spells. They seem to come oftener."

Andy's mind was on something else. "That's one swell girl who came out to marry Hy West. She gave me a dollar."

Belle made no attempt to hide her surprise. "Where is she now?"

Andy spoke without thinking. "Up in Hy's room."

Belle started to say something, then thought better of it. She gathered up the

47

shirts she had ironed and moved toward the back parlor.

She returned in less than a minute. "Andy —" there was nervousness in her voice — "your mother's worse. Get Doctor Condon right away."

"But —"

"Hurry!"

The boy gulped the rest of his milk and started toward the door.

"Run."

He ran then, suddenly frightened. He headed directly for Callahan's as the most likely place to find the doctor, but Condon was not there.

"You see him," he told the bartender, "tell him Ma is took real bad." Then he ran on down the street toward the 'dobe house which served as Condon's combination office and living quarters.

The sun-baked yard was surrounded by a high board fence to keep in the half-dozen snarling dogs. Andy paused at the gate. He did not like the dogs. Although he had tried, it was impossible to make friends with them. But Condon must be home, for there was a light shining through the front window.

He called, shouting Condon's name.

At the sound of his voice the dogs redoubled their clamor, rushing forward to leap against the gate in an effort to get out. The house door was pulled open and Condon roared at the dogs. They slunk back, their loud protest scaling downward to whines.

"What's wanted?" The doctor was an untidy, bulky figure in the yellow lamplight.

"It's Ma, she's took bad."

Condon answered him with a muffled curse. "Tell her to take a couple of her pills. I can't come now."

The boy was very frightened. "But you've gotta. Belle says she's real bad."

Condon was not impressed but he thought of something and laughed suddenly. "Get Hy West. He's at your place. Now's the time to find out what kind of a doctor he is." He slammed the door, thus cutting off the path of light which had lain across the yard. At once, the coyote dogs took up their brawling.

Andy hesitated, not knowing what to do. But it was plain that Condon was not coming, so he turned and ran back toward the Apache, muttering as he ran. He was very mad at Condon. He'd get even somehow, but he didn't quite know how.

He was crying as he burst into the lobby, tears which were a combination of his anger and his fear. He stopped when he saw Belle.

"Condon won't come."

Belle stared at him, not believing.

"He said to tell her to take her pills, and then he said to let Hy West doctor her."

It had not occurred to her to call West. The town was so used to depending on Condon. She ran up the stairs, knocked on West's door, then turned the knob and opened it quickly. She was startled to see West without his shirt, facing the strange girl.

Belle had forgotten that Andy had said the girl was in West's room, and for a moment surprise and embarrassment held her silent. Then the urgency of her need made her say,

"It's Mary. She's very sick and Condon won't come."

Of the three in the room West was the most at ease, the most businesslike. Laura had guessed at once that this was the girl over whom West had fought. She eyed her possible rival with careful attention, but West wasted no time. He caught up his medicine bag without bothering to put on his shirt and came into the hall.

"Where is she?"

"Back parlor."

He went down the stairs two at a time, with Belle following more slowly. She turned once and looked back. Laura Hall

50

was standing at the head of the stairs, her face expressionless. Then Belle forgot her as she followed West across the dining room and through the side door into the small parlor.

Mary Lawrence was past speech. The pain in her side was so acute that she could do nothing but moan. Belle gave West a careful but rapid description of the symptoms.

"This isn't her first spell. She gets dizzy and then sick at her stomach, and the pain is in her right side, low down."

"What's Condon say?"

She shrugged. "Indigestion. He gives her pills."

West had stripped back the covers, bared the abdomen and was prodding it gently as he watched the sick woman's face. He saw her wince, and turned toward the door where Andy stood nervously.

"Get Miss Hall." His voice was crisply professional. "Tell her I need her."

The boy ran toward the stairs. Belle said quickly, "What is it, Hy?"

West's words were shorter than he intended. "Heat some water, a lot of water. Clear off the kitchen table and get me all the light in there you can."

His manner frightened her. "You're —

51

you're going to operate?"

He nodded.

"What's the matter with her?"

"Her vermiform appendix, I think. I'm afraid it's already ruptured." He broke off as Laura came in, trailed by Andy, and then gave her his orders.

Laura was not excited. She was a competent nurse. "Why not use the Railroad Hospital?"

He said, "I haven't been there yet. I don't know what facilities they have and I haven't met Doctor Gruber. We haven't time to waste. Show Belle what to do in the kitchen. The table will have to be scrubbed, my instruments boiled. You'll find a can of ether in my bag. It will have to do."

She nodded, turning toward the kitchen. West told Andy, "I need a couple of strong men, the first you can find on the street."

The boy was gone almost before the doctor finished speaking. He came back in a few minutes with two railroad brakemen. West had found a blanket. He showed them how to use it as a stretcher, and helped them move the sick woman to the kitchen table.

The men left reluctantly. They did not like the idea that West was going to operate. "Where's Condon?" asked the taller of the two. "Maybe we should stop him."

His partner shook his head. "You stop him. That's the Orphan Kid. I heard to-night that he'd come back, and I guess he's a doctor from what they were saying at Callahan's. Besides, I'll bet Condon's drunk right now."

His friend did not take the bet. They went out and up the street, telling the news. In five minutes a crowd began to gather before the hotel.

Inside, West had ordered Andy from the kitchen and closed the dining room door. Then he went to work, and as he worked swiftly he thanked Providence that Laura was there to help him.

Had he had time he might have admired Belle's composure, but he had no time. This was the first operation the girl had ever wit-nessed, while he and Laura had participated in a hundred. But this was the first time he had acted entirely on his own without the hospital staff beside him.

His actions were nearly automatic, deft and rapid. He heard Belle's sharp drawn breath as he made his first incision, and then it was very quiet in the big square room.

He sighed with relief when he found that the appendix had not yet ruptured. But it was extremely swollen and inflamed. He removed it, cleansed the cavity and closed it neatly. But not until the sick woman had been swathed in rolled sheets and he had made a final check of her pulse did he look up.

Belle Callahan's face was dead white, and her even teeth had left sharp marks on the redness of her lower lip. Her eyes had darkened until they looked enormous and her voice was shaky.

"Is — is she all right?"

It was Laura who answered, speaking not to the girl but to West. "A very creditable operation, Doctor. I don't think Doctor Forbes could have done better himself."

The words brought a quick pleasure to West. As he washed his hands he felt that he had passed his first test. He thanked Laura by a quick kiss upon her cheek, then gathered up his instruments and packed them in his case.

Andy stood aside as they moved his mother through the wide doorway into the laundry where Belle had fixed a bed. The boy had recovered from his first fright, and his eyes showed the glint of hero worship.

"I was going to be a dispatcher, but I've changed my mind. Do you have to be very smart to be a doctor?"

West put a hand on his shoulder. "You're

54

smart enough, Andy. Are you willing to work?"

"I'll work," Andy said. "I'll really, truly work. You just wait and see."

chapter 5

Condon shut the door after sending Andy away. He turned to face the three Benton boys. Outside, the yammering of the dogs was already dying to dispirited whines. He had become so used to the racket that he did not hear them.

Bo Benton stood, his shirt removed, his scorched hands showing red and blistery, his back marred by a red blotch where the hot iron had touched him.

Vance and Fred were beyond the table, watching, and Condon looked at them in anger. "If that boy had found you hiding here the story would be all over town."

Vance grinned. Vance did not like Condon and took no trouble to hide his feelings. "I guess even the Bentons have a right to come to a doctor when they get burned." He grinned at Bo, who swore at him.

Condon glared, but did not answer as he started to examine Bo's back. The touch of his fingers was not gentle.

Bo winced. "For God's sake, Doc, take it easy."

Condon grunted. "Now you know what a cow feels like when you sear her hide with your running iron. Fred, go into the kitchen, heat a pail of water and dump in all the tea you can find. I want tea leaves, as many as there are, for a poultice."

Fred Benton disappeared into the kitchen. The doctor took a pair of scissors, punctured the blister and started to trim away the wrinkled skin.

The pain made Bo curse. "So help me, I'll run a gun barrel down the Orphan Kid's throat."

Vance laughed. Vance was two years older than Bo, and of all the Bentons he had been friendliest with West. "Way I heard it," he said, "it wasn't the Kid who swung that hot iron. It was the Callahan girl. Seems like she don't appreciate your courting."

Bo turned so quickly that the point of Condon's shears dug into his back. He yelped, then glowered at his grinning brother. "Keep your damn mouth out of my business."

Vance shrugged and went on mocking him. "Getting kind of uppity, aren't you, boy? I hear her old man is coining money. What are you after, the girl or the saloon?"

Bo started for Vance, but his brother

57

merely circled the table ahead of him. Condon laid down the shears deliberately.

"To hell with you. I can't dress your back if you waltz around like a traveling bear. Come back here. And if you don't want me to be digging one of Callahan's bullets out of your no-good hide you'll keep away from that girl."

Bo came back, grudgingly. Fred appeared from the kitchen carrying the bucket of soaked tea leaves. Condon picked up his shears and removed the rest of the loose skin, saying as he worked,

"None of you Bentons has a grain of sense. I curse the day I ever got mixed up with your family."

Fred's face darkened. He was the most quarrelsome of the Bentons and his face bore the scars of a dozen barroom fights. "You'd have starved to death without us, Doc."

Condon was fixing the tea-leaf poultice on Bo's back. He stopped, staring at Fred. "What's bothering you now?"

"Duke and Prince. They've been in prison nearly eight years. The Orphan Kid came back here today, free as air."

Condon said in a resigned tone, "I did all I could for them. I showed your mother the letter I got from the lawyer. We were hoping for a pardon by the new governor. No luck."

Fred said slowly, "You took your cut from every holdup we ever pulled. You owe it to the boys to get them out."

Condon finished fastening the poultice in place. He did not answer until it was secure. Then he said in a tired voice, "If Duke and Prince had listened to me, they wouldn't have held up that train and they wouldn't have been caught. And after they were, I brought a lawyer clear from Fort Smith to defend them."

"You kept Hy West from going to prison."

"His age and Dave Lawrence saved him. All I did was to bring Hy here when the court decided he couldn't go back to your ranch. He never even knew I was mixed up with you. There was nothing any of us could do for Duke and Prince. They were lucky not to get life."

"What difference does it make — twenty years — life? We're going to break them out."

Condon stared at him, realizing that this was not idle talk, that the Bentons actually planned to help their brothers escape. "How do you expect to do that?"

"You're going to figure that out," Fred told him. "Ma says you were all-fired smart,

59

planning our holdups. It should be a cinch for you to figure out how to free the boys."

Condon's temper was seldom even and it flared now. He knew that the Bentons were not normal; that they were ignorant and bigoted and had never seen a town larger than Soda Springs. For years their very name had terrorized this part of the country until they had an exaggerated opinion of what they could accomplish.

He glanced at Vance, knowing that he was the shrewdest member of the family. "Do you think this fool idea is possible, Vance?"

Vance shrugged. "When Ma gets an idea in her head, all the black powder in the world won't blow it out. You'd better start thinking Doc, or you'll be in trouble."

Condon laughed suddenly. "Do you think I'm a fool? I've been damn careful that no one suspected I was connected with you, or with your holdups. Don't threaten me. Who do you think would take your word against mine? I never held up a stage or stole a cow in my life."

"You killed Dave Lawrence." Fred was leaning across the table now, his dark eyes glowing, his mouth an ugly line. "You thought no one saw you that Christmas morning. You thought there was no one else in town awake when you stepped out of the alley and shot him in the back."

Condon's mouth went dry. He tried to speak and found that his stiff lips would not form the words. Fred saw the shock on the doctor's face and grinned wolfishly.

"Bo and I were sleeping in your stable that night. It was too cold when we quit drinking to ride home. We heard the dogs when you left and came down to see what was going on. We trailed you up the alley and we weren't fifteen feet from you when you poked your gun into Dave Lawrence's back."

Under the lamp light Condon's face glistened with sweat. A lesser man might have crumpled at learning suddenly that a secret he had kept closely guarded was known. The Lawrence affair had been his one act of real violence, and he had cursed himself a thousand times for giving way to his fear.

For Dave Lawrence's murder had grown out of Condon's fear that the sheriff had guessed his connection with the Bentons. He had never known what act of his had first aroused Lawrence's suspicion. But abruptly he became conscious that Lawrence was watching his every move, that each time he rode out of town, Lawrence trailed him. It was then that he had decided that the sheriff must die.

His plan had been simple, based on his knowledge of Lawrence's character. He had waited until a man wanted on a federal warrant was reported in the area; then he got word to Lawrence in the middle of the night that a stranger was hiding in the livery stable.

Lawrence had reacted as Condon knew he would. He came alone to investigate, walking along the deserted Railroad Avenue. And as he passed the alley, Condon stepped from the shadows to poke a gun against his back, to shoot him before he could turn.

By the time they had come to tell the doctor of the murder and call him in his official capacity as coroner, he was safely home in bed, apparently drunk. Neither the new sheriff nor the town marshal had made any real effort to find the murderer, believing it to be some chance rider who had had trouble with Lawrence, and Condon had nearly forgotten the crime.

Now he studied Fred's face. The Bentons had remained silent for over a year, waiting until they needed something from him before they used their knowledge. He could deny it of course. It would still be his word against theirs. But he could not afford to take the chance. It would be one thing to stand accused of planning a holdup in which he had taken no active part, and quite another to be charged with the cold-blooded killing of as popular a man as Dave Lawrence had been.

And other things would then come out. His long association with the Bentons . . .

He said tonelessly, "What is it you expect me to do?"

"Work up some way to get Duke and Prince out of prison."

"That's impossible."

"You'd better try." It was Fred. "We aren't fooling, and you know Ma. When she gets an idea in her head she's real impatient."

Condon wet his lips. He had to have time to think. He said, "You can't expect me to pull something out of my hat right now. Tell your Ma I'll come out to the ranch and we'll talk it over."

He watched them go with real relief. He had no idea what he meant to do. His first impulse was to pack his things and get away from Soda Springs as fast as he could ride. He could be a long way into the mountains before it dawned on the Bentons that he was gone.

He looked around the room. This was home, shabby as it was, and he was old. He did not want to change. Much as he mocked Soda Springs and its citizens, he had an acknowledged place here which he would never achieve anywhere else.

He sat down heavily before his desk and stared morosely at the tintype above the desk. It was the picture of a pretty, laughing woman, a pleasing picture. But it did not please Condon.

"Laugh," he snarled, talking to it as he sometimes did. "Laugh your head off, but I'm not through yet. You thought I was through once, and you were wrong. You're wrong now because I'm not finished. You just wait and see."

chapter 6

Bo was muttering to himself as they started down the dark street. Vance glanced at him curiously. "What's eating you?"

"The Kid's got my gun. Can't leave my gun in town. Whole darn town will laugh."

Fred said, "Let's go get it."

Vance turned in the saddle. "You crazy fool. Haven't you had enough trouble for one day?"

"I can take care of him," Bo promised. "If Belle hadn't burned me with that flatiron I'd have blown his fool head off."

"And hung for it."

"Look," Bo said. "Are you with me or not? You ride up to the hotel and tell the Kid I'm waiting for him down by the livery. Lend me your gun."

Vance shook his head. "I don't want any part of it."

"I'll go," Fred said, and swung his horse toward the hotel.

Vance said, "To hell with it." He turned and rode away. Bo watched him go in sullen silence. Then he thought of something. He still had no gun.

He swung around, intending to go back to Condon's and borrow one, but as he turned he saw his brother come down the hotel steps. He waited as Fred rode up.

Fred said, "He isn't there. He operated on the old lady. Then he went down to Callahan's for a drink."

Bo glanced up the street toward the saloon. "Let me have your gun."

Fred hesitated. "You aren't going in there by yourself?"

"Why not?"

"Callahan doesn't like trouble in there and he keeps a shotgun under the bar."

Bo swore. "Are you going to give me that gun or am I going to take it away from you?"

Fred shrugged and silently passed the gun to his brother. Bo dropped it into his empty holster. They rode toward the saloon in silence.

Gimble watched them from the far corner of the livery. The town's marshal had been looking for them most of the evening, wondering where they were. It wasn't that he wanted to see them. It was only that he would feel much safer once they were clear of town.

He saw them dismount before Callahan's, saw Fred pull the rifle from the boot beneath the stirrup. He frowned. "What in the devil?" he muttered aloud. Surely even the Bentons weren't crazy enough to attempt to hold up Callahan.

He swore. He wished someone else was town marshal. He wished he was a good hundred miles away.

At least no one knew where he was, and he did not mean to be present when the trouble started. He pulled his horse back into the deeper shadows, rode down the alley behind the livery, and so toward the end of town.

Before the saloon door, Fred Benton halted and levered a shell into the rifle chamber. Then he nodded. Bo pushed the bat-wing doors wide with a sweeping gesture of both hands, like a swimmer using the breast stroke, and in the next second was in the long room, Fred close behind.

The room was poorly filled, for it was late. Two tables of poker still carried on at the back of the room, but the bar was deserted aside from West who stood near the center, talking to Callahan.

He did not turn as Bo came in, but Callahan lifted his head and at once sensed danger. He was too old a hand not to recognize the signs and he said, hardly moving his lips, his voice little more than a whisper, "Watch it, Doc."

As he spoke his eyes dropped to West's belt. He noticed the absence of any weapon and he frowned.

West lifted his eyes to the mirror. He saw Bo standing inside the door. Fred was at his back, and he saw the rifle in Fred's hands.

He knew at once that their arrival was no accident. Even the Bentons did not enter a saloon carrying a rifle unless they were after someone, and he guessed that that someone was him. Under his breath he cursed himself for being so careless as to come out alone and unarmed. His years in the East had lulled him into a feeling of false security.

He stood there, not turning, waiting for what was going to happen, powerless to prevent it. He sensed that Callahan was reaching under the bar, and when the big saloonkeeper straightened he held a sixgun almost hidden in his big hand.

This he slid across to West, keeping it screened from the view of the men behind West's body. Hy reached out and slipped it under his belt. As he did so he glanced again in the mirror.

Fred had halted just inside the door. He stood with his rifle held down alongside his right leg as if he thought that by so standing

68

no one in the saloon would notice it.

Bo came on, moving carefully. His legs were stiff. He had pulled the wrappings from his burned hand and it hung claw-like at his side, below the butt of the holstered gun.

He advanced until less than ten feet separated him from West. There he stopped, standing with his feet a little apart, his shoulders slightly hunched.

"Kid."

West said, "What is it?" He was conscious that the players at the card tables in the rear had ceased their games and were turning to watch.

"I've come for my gun."

"Oh, that." West sounded surprised. "Why of course." He turned then, and to the men watching from the rear tables it seemed that he whirled. As he came around his long fingered right hand dropped to his belt. The gun seemed to grow into his hand. He jumped then, as Fred started to bring up his rifle. He jammed the gun hard into Bo's stomach, almost knocking the wind out of the youngest Benton.

Bo had started to draw as West turned, but the gun was hardly clear of the holster when the barrel of West's weapon jarred into his belt line. He stopped, frozen.

West said tonelessly, "Let it drop, Bo."

Benton stared into the doctor's eyes, finding them cold, a little mocking, but utterly unyielding. He knew West well enough to sense that if he failed to obey, the gun against his stomach would explode.

Suddenly he was scared. His burned fingers released their grip and the gun slid from his grasp to thud onto the scarred floor at his feet.

Fred Benton had his rifle half raised, but Bo's body was between him and his target. For a minute he hesitated, and in that minute Callahan took a hand in the game, poking the twin barrels of his Greening across the bar top so that they covered Fred Benton.

"Put it down, Fred."

Benton said savagely, "We won't forget this, Callahan."

"Remember it then." The big Irishman was unmoved. "Any time you think you or your brothers can walk into my place and shoot holes in my mirror you better think again. Lay the rifle on the floor and get out."

For an instant it seemed that Fred would refuse. Then with a muttered oath, he threw the gun from him so that it clattered against the wall as it fell. Without even looking toward it Fred Benton swung on his heel, knocked the doors aside and plunged out into the night.

West used one hand to swing Bo around and push him after his retreating brother. He followed him clear to the door, and stood watching above the bat-wings as the Bentons mounted and spurred furiously out of town.

Not until he was certain that they were gone did he come back toward the bar, gathering the rifle and sixgun up from the floor as he passed.

He dumped them on the bar and added the gun which Callahan had slid to him. "Thanks. Sorry you had to get in trouble with the Bentons because of me."

"Scum," Callahan said, depositing the firearms under the counter. "If the people in this town had the guts of rabbits we'd have run the Bentons out of the country long ago. Drink?" He did not wait for an answer, but poured whisky for two. "Why the devil did you come back to this mess anyhow?"

West didn't answer. He drank his whisky and then with a nod turned out into the night.

The following day the town's single paper asked the same question. Why had Doctor West come back to Soda Springs? It was seldom that Bert Borus, the editor, had much to write about, and he spread himself. He had pieced together most of the story, the fight West had had with Bo in the hotel kitchen, West's operation on Mary Lawrence, Laura's arrival to marry West, and the brush in Callahan's saloon.

From there the editor went backward, reminding his readers that this was the boy who had once been called the Orphan Kid, who had only escaped going to prison with Duke and Prince Benton because of his youth; recalling how Doctor Condon had taken the boy, how the boy had run away East and studied to be a doctor, and how he had now returned to serve as an assistant at the Railroad Hospital.

On the whole the story pictured West in a favorable light, but it did point out that he had been raised by the Bentons, that as a boy he was sullen and quarrelsome, and that he had had two fights the very day he returned.

The town read and divided as most towns do. Some citizens were for leaving West alone. Others, including the minister of one church and the elder of another, met and decided that it was both illegal and an outrage that a man who should by rights be in prison was allowed to practice medicine in Soda Springs. These carried their complaint to the division superintendent.

Dr. Franz Gruber, head of the Railroad Hospital, read the paper as he stood at the bar in Callahan's having his morning drink.

Gruber did not like Soda Springs, or the hospital, or the patients he was supposed to serve, and he would not have read the paper had not his eye caught the headline:

NEW DOCTOR
FOR RAILROAD HOSPITAL

Gruber was a stuffy man, not quite middle-aged. He had graduated with honors in Vienna and had looked forward to a brilliant career. But drink and serious trouble with a woman forced him to flee the continent, and he might have starved had not a chance acquaintance in New York told him that the Pacific Railroad was building a chain of hospitals through the west and having difficulty finding enough doctors to staff them.

When he was sent to Soda Springs the empty, barren country depressed him, the violence of the people frightened him, and only fear that he would not find another job made him stay.

His hands trembled as he read the headline, for he thought at first that he was being removed. Then, after he had read the whole article, he was horrified. His new assistant was a former outlaw, a train robber. He laid the paper on the bar and hurriedly left the saloon.

And the first glimpse Gruber had of his new assistant was not reassuring. West was big. He weighed a good thirty pounds more than Gruber, and none of it was fat. His eyes were level and direct and unyielding, and Gruber had to steel himself to speak.

"You're new," he said, "so you may not know the strict company rule. None of us are allowed any private practice. The railroad doesn't want to antagonize the doctors in the towns along the right-of-way."

West said shortly, "Condon was called and refused to come. The operation could not be postponed."

Gruber flushed at his tone, but managed to say in a level voice, "It's nice to have you here. We will now keep the hospital open through the night. We will alternate. Every other week you will take the night shift, and it will also be part of your work to ride the wrecking train in case of accident. Now, I'll show you around." He led West first into the second office, then through the ward. The hospital was nearly empty, the only bed patients being a brakeman whose crushed leg had been removed, and two section hands who had gotten into a fight on a work train and fallen to the ballast, lacerating themselves but breaking no bones.

West was seized by a feeling of depression. He had come here to work, to learn. A new doctor learned only by experience. And there did not seem to be enough here to keep one man occupied. He watched while Gruber examined the brakeman's stump. He could find no fault with Gruber's surgery, but it was evident that the administration at the hospital was very lax and he smelled the heavy odor of whisky upon Gruber's breath.

The floors were dirty and the kitchen worse. It was with a feeling of relief that he left, promising to report at six that evening.

Outside he found Andy and a small, sandy-haired boy waiting for him. Andy introduced his companion as Sam Dillon.

"He's going to be a doctor too," Andy explained. "Sandy does everything I do."

West nodded, his mind busy on other things. "The world's a big place. It can use a lot of doctors."

Sam's voice had a piping quality. "We were going to be dispatchers yesterday," he explained, "but Andy says being a doctor is much more important. Does a doctor make more than a dispatcher?"

"Some do."

Sam considered, then brightened. "Say, have you still got your guns? My Pa says that when you were a boy you were real fast with them."

West shook his head, and disappointment registered on the faces of both his companions.

"I've got my father's," Andy said. "Ma don't know it, but I've got them in my bureau. I practice with them real often."

West didn't answer. He could think of nothing appropriate to say.

"Would you show me how to use them some time?"

He stopped then, looking down into Andy's face. "I don't think I'd better," he said slowly. "I wore my guns to school once when I wasn't too much older than you are, and I almost got into bad trouble. Your father took them away from me, and he made me promise that I wouldn't wear them again. He showed me that guns were only made for enforcing the law, not breaking it."

Neither boy answered and after a moment they moved on down the street toward the hotel, passing a dozen people as they progressed.

One or two nodded casually to West. Several merely stared. The rest ignored him. No one spoke until they rounded the corner and came face to face with Bruce Gimble and Al DeMember, the sheriff.

West stopped, for the men were standing side by side, blocking the sidewalk. He started to smile, then let his lips straighten as he saw no welcome in either of their faces.

Gimble's first glance had been at West's waist as if he had hoped to catch the young doctor wearing a gun and therefore breaking the town ordinance. Then he saw the two boys and scowled at them.

"You kids get out of here."

Both Andy and Sam Dillon were taken by surprise. They stared at him, not moving, and red crept up under his deep tan. "Hear me, you move!"

West said mildly, "What's the matter? They aren't doing anything wrong."

Gimble glared at him. "I'll be the judge of that. We want to talk to you and we don't want them hanging around. Now, get."

They got, retreating reluctantly, looking back across their shoulders. He waited until they rounded the corner. DeMember had not spoken. He was a big man, placid and unhurried.

Gimble said, "A lot of our better citizens

don't take kindly to you coming back here. They don't think a train robber will make a good doctor."

West said calmly, "The railroad doesn't object. The Chicago office knew my history before they hired me. I'm not going into general practice, Gimble. I'm working for the railroad."

The marshal scowled at him, baffled. He was not a bright man and his mind worked slowly. "And you're a trouble maker," he said. "You hadn't been in town five hours before you were in trouble."

"What kind of trouble?"

Gimble was growing angry. "Don't try and play innocent. You had a fight with Bo Benton, didn't you? I tell you, West, we don't want you here. We want you out of town."

Hy said idly, "Have you ordered Bo to stay out? He started it."

Gimble's face gained color. He was very conscious of his fear of the Bentons. "That's different," he muttered. "The Bentons kind of belong here."

"So do I," West said. "Or have you forgotten?"

He had been trying to hold his temper, having expected something like this from the first. They were standing close together and Gimble made a mistake.

"I mean it," he said, and dropped his hand to his gun. He actually did not intend to draw it; he was only trying to emphasize his words. But Hy West's reaction was instinctive. The moment Gimble's right hand dropped, West's left shot out. He caught the marshal's wrist in a vise-like grip and crossed his right to Gimble's jaw.

The marshal fell. As he went down West jerked the gun from Gimble's holster. Swinging on the balls of his feet, he jammed the heavy barrel into the stomach of the amazed sheriff.

DeMember gasped, the air partly driven out of him. He was a man who avoided unnecessary violence at all times. Not as able a man as Dave Lawrence had been, nor as smart, he still had little love for Gimble and had not realized what the marshal had in mind.

He spread both his big hands out, well away from his body, palms down to show that he wanted no part of this. "You didn't have to poke my stomach in, Hy. Gimble was out of line."

West had recovered from his quick, momentary flash of anger and embarrassment crept into his voice. "Sorry, Al. He caught me unexpectedly."

"Which was what he intended." DeMember's voice was dry.

West reversed the marshal's gun and extended it to the sheriff, butt first. He did not look at Gimble who was getting slowly to his feet. He moved on past the sheriff, knowing that the man turned as he passed and watched him, muttering under his breath. He neither knew nor cared what DeMember said. He was shaking a little from reaction by the time he entered the hotel.

The lobby was quiet and he paused inside its shadows to hold up his right hand, looking at it curiously. It was trembling and he smiled wryly. I've got to get hold of myself, he thought. I'm letting the town get me down. I knew that there would be trouble when I came back, but I pictured nothing like this.

He went on into the kitchen then, expecting to find Laura Hall with Mrs. Lawrence. She was nowhere in sight. Belle Callahan was alone, seated at the kitchen table. She looked up and put one finger to her lips.

"Mary's asleep."

"How is she?"

"The nurse said she was all right." She accented the word "nurse" slightly and he gave her a sharp glance. Obviously, Belle didn't like Laura. It was so very easy to tell when Belle did not like someone. There was almost no pretense about her.

He said in defense, "I'm very glad Laura was here last night. I would have hated to operate without her." He knew he was making an effort to justify Laura, and was surprised that he felt the necessity. "Where is she now?"

"She went to lie down. She was up half the night."

He nodded and asked for a cup of coffee. She brought it to the table and sat down beside him. "So you aren't going to stay, Hy?"

He looked at her in surprise. "Not stay? Where did you get the idea?"

"Miss Hall told me. We had quite a talk. I don't think your Miss Hall likes me much. She asked me a lot of questions about you. I think she sensed a romance between us."

He grinned, stirring the sugar into the coffee. "Did you tell her that you were too smart to have anything to do with me?"

Her smile in return was faint. "I agreed with her that you were a damn fool to come back to Soda Springs. She told me about the offer from Doctor Forbes. Why did you come back here, Hy?"

It was the question he had been asking himself all morning, but he temporized. "Maybe I got homesick. I've been away a long time."

She said, almost roughly, "Stop evading. I know why you came back. Even your Laura knows. Don't tell me you aren't as smart as we are."

His grin widened. "All right, Miss Portia, tell me — why did I come back?"

"Because," she said, "you're a chuckle-headed son of a long-tailed mule."

He laughed outright. "Such language."

"I learned my language in the army," she told him, "and that's an old expression of my father's. He reserved it for each new set of green recruits. Don't you remember how shocked the teachers were at the way I swore?"

He did remember. "You've developed into quite a lady."

"Stop it," she said. "We never kidded each other, Hy, even when we fought."

"No," he said, "we never kidded each other." He looked at her and felt a sudden warmness which he had not experienced since his return. He was easy with Belle Callahan; that was the word, easy. With her he never had to pretend. With her he could relax the defensive mask which he had built

82

up to protect himself against the world.

He tried to analyze the reason for this. Perhaps it went a long way back. Perhaps it was because out of the whole school he and Belle had been the two outsiders, the ones whom the other children looked on a little askance. They'd both had chips on their shoulders, knowing that they were not accepted: he, because he was associated with the Bentons, she because her father had been an army sergeant, and now ran a saloon.

"That's the only reason I'm talking to you now," she said. "Because we've never kidded ourselves and it's a little late to begin. It's none of my damn business, Hy, but somehow I feel a little responsible for you."

He looked at her in surprise and she colored faintly. "You don't need to begin to get worried. I decided a long time ago that marriage was not for me. I saw what it did to my mother, and to the other women on the post. This is a man's world, Hy. The women sit at home and knit."

He had a momentary vision of Laura. No matter what else she did, Laura would never sit at home.

Belle was not smiling now. Words had never come too easily for this girl and she was having trouble making her reasoning plain to him.

"There's nothing for you in Soda Springs. You can stay here for twenty years and without a miracle they will never accept you — and you are a person who needs to be accepted. I remember how hurt you were, down inside, when the school kids used to call you an outlaw and a train robber. You wanted to fight back because you were hurt. But the more you fought the farther apart you set yourself, the higher you built the wall which separated you from the town."

He knew she was right and he found a moment to marvel at her ability to understand. But then he realized that the understanding came out of her own deep bitterness.

"What you're saying applies to you as well as to me."

"It does."

"Then why don't you take your own advice and get out?"

"Because I'm a coward." She said this frankly. "I'm not happy here. At times I'm lonely, and I always have the feeling that if I went away, things might be better. But I'm afraid to put it to the test. I have no training. I've never been a hundred miles away from here. What little I do have is centered in the

84

Springs. But you are different. You've already made the break. You have your training and your future before you. You have a pretty girl to marry and a chance to work with Doctor Forbes. Again I tell you — stop being a long-tailed mule. You came back here to prove something, to prove to yourself that you can break down the prejudice against you in this town. You can't. People resent those who are different from them in any way."

"I'm not entirely sure."

"Because you won't face facts as they are, because you hate to admit that you've been wrong for six long years. Nothing has changed here since you left. If you don't believe it, get a horse and ride out to the Benton ranch."

"An idea, that."

"A poor one, but it might bring you to your senses. A look at the house where you were raised and the people you were raised with might show you how very far you've traveled in six years. Go on, go. Don't worry about Mary. Miss Hall's here and although I freely admit I don't like her I think she's competent with the sick."

He went then, and as he crossed the lobby, he knew a sudden eagerness which he had not expected. On the porch outside he

85

was stopped by Andy and Sam Dillon. Andy was bubbling with excitement.

"It's all over town," he said. "The way you knocked Bruce Gimble down. I'll bet that will make people stop and think. I'll bet from now on they'll be careful to let you alone."

That, West thought as he descended the two steps and moved up the sidewalk toward the livery, was the trouble. Everything that had happened to him since his return seemed to be building the wall higher. He had wanted to come back to Soda Springs to gain respect from the people who had once sneered at him. He realized that fully now, and these early setbacks troubled him all the more because of his knowledge.

It was such a nebulous thing, and yet so very important to his self esteem. He might run away, back to Doctor Forbes and the hospital, telling himself that the fools who made up the population of the town did not matter. But he was as honest with himself as he had tried to be with Belle. They did matter. Even a fool like Bruce Gimble mattered. At the moment a word of grudging praise from Gimble would be more important than a citation from the President. He smiled wryly.

The horse which Wentworth rented him was a bay. It had been in the corral for days and it wanted to run. Once free of town he made no effort to curb it. Fast riding gave him a sense of freedom which he had not known for a long time. The empty country stretched away toward the distant hills, limitless, unhampered by buildings or fence.

The high, dry air was so clear that the mountains stood out against the sky like cutouts, yet three-dimensional and massive in their towering hugeness.

He knew each foot of this wild land. The whole place was a maze of trails, and the land here was so dry that tracks which had been made months before seemed to have the clarity of yesterday.

He rode, and the horse, having had its blowout run, settled into the steady gait which would carry it on for miles and miles. The country roughened, and spurs of rocky shoulders ran out now into the uneven plain. The trail climbed, and the vegetation altered, and now there were tiny streams in the canyon bottoms, racing torrents which would lose themselves to the south in the ever thirsty sand.

He knew a sudden urge to keep riding, into the mountains, beyond the mountains, until he had completely lost himself, and a desire never to see Soda Springs again, to leave the Railroad Hospital behind, to forget Condon, and the Bentons, and even Laura Hall.

But he knew it was not for him. Some people were fiddle-footed. Some people could shed responsibilities as they would remove an old coat, but this was not for him. He knew that he would go back, that he would stay in the Springs, stay there until he had whipped the town or it had whipped him.

Side trails were splitting off to right and left now, reaching out like the ribs of a fan into the small mountain meadows where the solitary ranches hid their weathered buildings. He had known these people. They were like the Bentons, suspicious of strangers, violent, resentful of those who chose to live in town.

Theirs was a marginal existence. They hunted a little, ran a few cattle, and were not above branding a stray calf or running off a few horses.

An unarmed stranger was not safe in these hills, and he had armed himself, wearing Bo Benton's gun in a borrowed holster, carrying the rifle he had borrowed from Wentworth under his knee.

It was not that he expected trouble, yet he

knew that if he ran into Bo Benton or Fred there might well be another fight. He had no intention of ducking them. This ride was a kind of test. He could not remain in this country indefinitely and quarrel with the Bentons every time they met. He wanted to talk to Ma. A word from Ma Benton would curb her warlike sons quicker than anything else.

But just as he reached the mouth of the canyon which led to the Benton ranch he had a sudden impulse and turned the horse into a steep, rocky trail which led up through the timber to the canyon rim over-looking the Benton house.

At the top the trail ended abruptly in a little promontory and he stepped down, set-ting the horse free to graze on the scattered tufts of mountain grass.

He walked to the rim and stood looking down on the roofs of the place which had been his home, the only home he could re-member. It was a typical mountain ranch, the house of logs, its corral of poles, its sheds and outbuildings grass-roofed. It sat at the head of a bottle-shaped canyon, facing the neck, some two hundred acres, fenced by the natural rise of the canyon sides. It was seldom that anyone save the Bentons rode into the valley.

But even as West reached the rim he saw a horseman coming up the trail through the lower canyon. The rider must have been fairly close behind him on the main trail. The thought crossed his mind that the rider could have been following him, but then he dismissed the idea as ridiculous. There was no reason for anyone to follow him out from Soda Springs.

He hunkered down, idly picking a stem of the dried grass and twisting it between his lips. He had always liked this spot as a boy, and he had climbed here often to escape the turmoil in the valley below.

His eyes centered on the rider as the horse climbed the steep pitch of the lower canyon and the man grew in size as he approached. There was something familiar about him, but at the distance West failed to realize who it was until he reached the corral fence and stepped down to walk onward toward the house. Then recognition came. There was no mistaking Dr. Condon's walk.

Someone came from the house porch to meet the doctor and they paused for an instant in the center of the yard, then turned and moved back to the house.

West waited motionless. His first thought was that someone in the house below him was sick. He wondered who it was and decided that it must be the mother.

And suddenly he had his idea. It pleased him. He would simply walk in, a doctor, offering his aid. Bo must have told Ma Benton about his return, but she would still be surprised to see this boy whom she had raised, entering as a doctor.

The stream ran down on his right, dropping over the rim in a series of short rapids to fall the last hundred feet to the canyon floor in a direct drop which landed in a round, deep pool above the house.

Beside the stream zigzagged the path. It was a footpath only, too narrow and steep for any horse, but he had climbed it many times as a youngster. If he rode back to the canyon mouth it would take almost an hour to reach the house. By the path, he could make it in less than ten minutes.

He started downward, still carried forward by impulse, feeling his way cautiously. The going was steeper than he had remembered and he sighed with relief when he reached the level ground beside the pool.

The woodshed was between him and the house and he came around it with a curious feeling of nostalgia. His memory naturally inclined to retain the nice things which had happened rather than the bad, and he had not been too unhappy at this ranch.

The yard itself was filled with remembered things: the tree from which he used to mount his horse before he was large enough to reach the stirrup; the old tin target which he and Vance and Bo had trained their first guns on, still tacked to the woodshed door; the old milk house beside the stream where Ma had cooled her butter crocks; the open forge where Prince had showed him how to cinch on a shoe.

He climbed the pole fence and came up into the main yard, and then he stopped suddenly. Vance Benton had come from behind the house and Vance was carrying a rifle in the cradle of his arm.

Hy waited for a cheerful greeting. He had always felt closer to Vance than all the rest. He had even looked up to the older boy.

But the greeting he expected failed to come. There was no smile to twist Vance's thin-lipped mouth, no welcome in his dark, flat eyes.

"What are you following Condon for?"

Hy West could not have been more surprised if he had been accused of stealing drugs from the Railroad Hospital.

He started to grin, thinking it a joke. Then his grin faded as Vance shifted the rifle. "Give me your gun," Vance said.

West had the impulse to pull Bo's gun

and take his chances with Vance. But he had not come here to fight. His intention had been to make his peace with Ma Benton.

He said slowly, "Bo's in there, and spoiling for my blood."

"Then why'd you come?" Vance stared at him coldly.

West told him then. He said, "I wanted to see Ma. I haven't seen her for over six years, and I wanted to patch things up with Bo. What the hell, Vance, I'm going to stay in this country. I don't want to carry on a feud with you Bentons. After all, you're the only family I ever had."

There was still suspicion in Vance's eyes. "Then why'd you try and sneak in the back way? Why didn't you ride up the canyon?"

West tried to explain. "Remember how we used to play, up there on the rim? I suddenly thought of it as I rode in, and took the hill trail. Then from the rim I saw Condon. I thought someone was sick, so I came down to help."

He watched Vance's face as he spoke, trying to decide if he had convinced him. He couldn't be sure. Vance said, "You'd better give me that gun."

West drew it slowly and extended it butt first. Vance glanced at it and his thin lips curved a little. "Bo's?"

West nodded.

"I'll tell him you rode out to return it. That may quiet him a little. At any rate I'll see he doesn't start anything as long as you aren't armed."

chapter 7

Ma Benton was exactly five feet tall and never in her life had she weighed more than ninety pounds. Her husband had been six-feet-two and every one of her five sons stood over six feet.

But she was the brains of the family, and always had been. Hers was the driving power which stirred them into activity, and although all the boys were now full grown she still tried to dominate them as she had dominated them as children.

Condon had always found her both interesting and amusing, and it had been for amusement as much as anything else that he first became involved in the Bentons' illegal enterprises.

He was a man turned bitter by life, who resented what organized society had done to him, and he had begun to take a sardonic revenge in plotting the minor crimes which the Benton boys and their wild-riding neighbors carried out.

That he had gotten involved far deeper than he intended was due to carelessness and accident, and to his ever increasing drinking, and the fact that his practice hardly managed to pay his enormous bar bills. As he grew older he had become more and more careless, but when Duke and Prince finally waxed ambitious and planned the holdup of the express car with its box which was reported to contain over thirty thousand dollars, he had drawn back.

He, far more clearly than they, understood that there was a vast difference between holding up an isolated stage and robbing a few passengers, and holding up the through limited and thus bringing down upon themselves a flood of railroad detectives and Pinkerton men.

But although he had refrained from having any part in the holdup planning, he had done his best, once Duke, Prince, and Hy West had been captured, to secure them the lightest sentences possible. Although never appearing openly, he had arranged for the lawyer from Fort Smith, and paid for the defense out of his own pocket, knowing that if he refused the Bentons would turn on him like hungry animals.

But now, even though he had done everything a man could, they were yapping at his heels, threatening him with exposure for Dave Lawrence's murder.

There was no arguing with the Bentons. Their ignorance was so enormous that plain logic made not the slightest appeal. He had drunk himself into a stupor, trying to think of some method which might stand even a slight chance of freeing the two brothers from the Territorial Prison, and had thought of nothing. But he dared not admit to the Bentons that there was anything to which he could not somehow find an answer. His only hold on the unruly family came of their belief that once he really put his mind to it he could figure out anything.

He had taken half a dozen drinks and was sweating profusely as he dismounted at the corral fence and moved up across the sloping yard. He still had no answer, but the liquor had given him courage. He would tell them he had formulated a rough plan, but that it would take several weeks to develop. In that time anything could happen, and Condon's alcohol-soaked brain told him that anything was better than a showdown now.

Fred came out into the yard to meet him, and together they mounted to the sagging porch and entered the square front room. Bo was seated beyond the stove. He did not even bother to get up.

Ma Benton said, "So you decided to

come out." She sounded sarcastic. She had a voice like the high pitched call of a water bird. Condon knew at once that he was in for a bad time. He pressed his big, beefy hands against his throbbing temples.

"Look, Ma, I —"

"You're no good, Doc." She said it without emphasis as if she were stating a well accepted fact which brooked no argument. "You never were any good, and you've been lording it high and mighty around here for a long time, telling us what to do. Well now, it's our turn to tell you."

Condon looked around. Fred had followed him into the room and shut the door. Fred was grinning.

The mother went on. "I guess the boys laid it on the line last night. I guess they scared you or you wouldn't have come busting out here this morning."

"I've always come when you've asked me to." He tried dignity.

She sneered at him. "So now I'm asking you to figure a way to break Prince and Duke out of that prison. Have you figured it out yet?"

He said slowly, conscious that her round, black eyes were watching him intently, "I been thinking about it. I thought about it all last night."

"You're a liar." She was staring at his puffy face. "You drank yourself stupid last night, Doc, like you usually do. But you're going to think about it now."

"I tell you I've got to have time —"

"I've been doing some thinking myself," she said tartly. "Maybe I ain't as smart as you, Doc, but I get ideas. For one thing I know that prison doctor calls you in when they got sickness up there. That gets you on the inside. Maybe you could take some guns in to the boys. Maybe they could do the rest themselves."

He was horrified. The last thing in the world he wanted was to be involved directly in a prison break. "I couldn't do that," he said. "They search me every time." This of course was not true, but he had to say something and it was the first thing which came into his mind.

"Then how do we get them some guns?"

He shrugged. "I told you I'm working on it. I'll think of something." They might be able to fight their way out with guns, but he doubted it. "But once they're outside they'll need help."

She was not concerned. "That's easy. The boys have enough friends in these hills."

"And we'll have to arrange to get them across the border."

She was startled. "Mexico? Why can't they come back here? There are plenty of places to hide in these hills."

He tried to be patient with her ignorance. "When Prince and Duke break out every able-bodied man in the Territory will be in the posse, and every soldier from the fort. Don't forget, that is a federal prison and these hills will be combed until a rabbit couldn't escape. And it will take money, a lot of money, to stay safe below the line. You'll have to pay off the authorities down there."

"We'll get the money." It was Fred.

Condon glanced at him, wondering what foolishness was cooking up in Fred's brain. Then he shrugged, looking back at the old woman.

"Remember," he warned, "this will take time to arrange. It can't happen tomorrow or the next day."

Her face hardened. "It better not take too long. The boys warned you they'd talk to Al DeMember, and they weren't fooling. You fail us on this, Doc, and I'll live to see you dance at the end of a rope."

She broke off as steps sounded on the porch. Everyone turned. Hy West came into the room with Vance at his heels, still carrying his rifle.

"Look what I found climbing down the cliff," Vance said. "He claims he rode out just to say hello to you, Ma."

Condon was staring at West with bulging eyes. Bo rose with a muttered curse and kicked his chair out of the way. Fred Benton held his place beside the door, not moving.

West looked around. His first thought was, There's something out of the ordinary going on here. They don't look natural and Ma isn't sick. No one is sick. What is Condon doing here and why are they so nervous? It isn't like them to be nervous. Ordinarily they don't know what nerves are.

He looked at Condon with renewed attention. He had never understood the man. He had never solved the mystery of why Condon, of all people, should have taken him in after the train robbery. Condon had never actually mistreated him, any more than Condon had mistreated the coyote dogs. In fact, Condon when sober had talked to him now and then about medicine.

That had first captured his interest. He realized, without knowing how he knew, that under his drunken exterior Condon had a real love for his profession.

But Condon had so seldom been sober, and Condon drunk was an entirely different person. Hy had hated the old doctor when

101

he was drunk. He had kept out of his way as much as possible.

For Condon's tongue was razor sharp, and he spared no one. He had railed at the boy then, calling him ignorant, stupid, uneducated. He had told him over and over that he could not be trusted. At times it had seemed almost as if Condon had hated him, had seen in him something which Condon despised.

He looked at the doctor now, wondering how Condon felt about him actually, and saw only fear in the prominent eyes. Condon was afraid. You could almost smell the fear within the room. Condon was afraid, and not of him. It must be of the Bentons, and that hardly made sense.

Condon had sometimes railed against the Bentons, but West had never thought too much about it. He had been too occupied with his own misery. He had supposed that it was merely the doctor's way of trying to wean him from the influences of his foster home.

Ma was looking at him in that studying way of hers. He remembered the same look when he had been very small. He had learned early that there was no good in trying to lie to her. She could ferret out a lie faster than anyone he had ever known. She seemed to have a sixth sense which warned her when he had not been telling the truth. She had whipped him in those days, using a piece of an old harness strap, but she had not whipped him more than she did her own sons. She had been very impartial about that.

"So you came back," she said. "I never expected to see you again."

"I came back," he said, and wondered at his own lack of feeling. This woman had raised him, had fed him, and clothed him and at times shown him a certain amount of kindness. And in those days he had not wanted to be an outsider. He had wanted to be a Benton.

Bo never let him forget that he was an outsider. Vance never mentioned the fact, and the older boys had usually ignored him unless he got in their way.

The Bentons were bound together by a tight, rigid clan instinct which had little or nothing to do with real affection. And he as a boy had wanted affection. He knew this now. In medical school he had used himself as a kind of case history, trying to analyze his own emotions, and he had realized in a half sentimental way that the Bentons were the only family he would ever have.

But seeing them now brought only a

quick curiosity as to why they had gathered in this room, as to what Condon was doing at the ranch, as to what made them so suspicious of his own presence.

"I came back," he repeated, and put a smile upon his lips although he felt no mirth, "because I wanted you to know that one of your boys went and got educated as a doctor."

"One of my boys?" she repeated it to herself as if the words came as a surprise. "At least you've grown. You used to be a puny little runt."

"You take the credit," he said, and meant the words. "There never was a better cook than you."

That touched her. Ma Benton had always prided herself upon her cooking. She wiped her hands on her apron and relaxed a little.

"You didn't give me too much trouble." She had softened as much as she would ever soften. "You didn't give me as much trouble as some of my own, but I didn't expect you to bother to ride out." A trace of bitterness crept into her voice. "I thought you were all through with the Bentons."

He said quickly, "I couldn't come before I went away. The judge said that if I ever came back to the ranch I'd have to go to prison. I was on parole."

She didn't understand the word. She had never understood why Prince and Duke had been locked up and this boy freed, and remembering it hardened her mouth. She did not blame him for their being in prison, but she resented him because he was free.

"So you had to come back, spying around?" He sensed the renewed suspicion in her tone and said, "Would you call it spying if Vance had been away and suddenly came home?"

"Vance belongs here."

That, he thought, was the basic difference, the thing which Belle had tried to make him see, the reason she had sent him to the ranch. In the Bentons' eyes he did not belong, just as in the eyes of the Soda Springs people he was an outsider to be treated with constant suspicion.

"All right," he said. "I guess I made a mistake in coming. I won't bother you. But I'm going to stay in Soda Springs, and I don't want to have to fight Bo and Fred every time we meet."

Bo said angrily, "It's damn lucky Callahan was there with his shotgun last night."

West looked at him. He had the impulse to remind Bo that he had already shoved a gun into Bo's stomach before Callahan had moved with the shotgun. He didn't.

Vance said, "Trouble with Bo is that he thinks you're trying to take Belle away from him. Truth is, she won't even look in Bo's direction."

Bo's anger switched to Vance. "That's a damn lie."

Fred could not resist saying, "At least she put her brand on Bo yesterday."

Bo had forgotten West in his anger against his two brothers. He turned and went through the kitchen door, slamming it behind him.

Ma shrugged. "You and Bo will have to work it out. You and he never got along too good."

That was true, and he realized from the flatness of her tone that he would get no help from her. He thought of something else.

"I never asked you who I was, Ma, where you got me, or who my parents are."

She looked at him for a long moment, and when she spoke her tone was curiously gentle. "You wouldn't be any happier if I told you, Kid. Now go on out with Vance. I want to talk to Doc."

He was dismissed, and he knew the dismissal was final.

"Good-bye, Ma."

She did not even answer, and he went back to the porch with Vance at his side. Fred followed them, closing the door. Fred seemed to hold no rancor for the preceding night.

"How was it in Chicago, Kid?"

"All right," West said.

There was envy in Fred's voice. "Some day I'm going to take me a trip. Some day I'm going to see that town. I hear it's really something."

He did not follow them across the yard, but Vance stayed at West's side and West noticed that Vance had left his rifle in the house. They reached the foot of the cliff and he paused. "No need for you to climb, Vance."

Vance shrugged. "Haven't gone up there in years. Might be fun."

West couldn't decide whether Vance was following him to make certain he actually rode away, or merely for companionship. They reached the rim, both a little short of breath, and turned to look back down at the buildings below.

He did not offer his hand, and Vance did not expect it. He had been much closer to Vance than the other brothers, but now there was an air of reserve between them.

He caught his horse and stepped into the saddle.

"See you in town."

Vance looked up at him. "Watch out for Bo. He's crazy where Belle is concerned."

West nodded. "For your information, I'm not marrying Belle. I'm marrying a girl from Chicago."

Vance shrugged. "None of my business." He was silent, considering. "What in hell did you come back here for? There's nothing in this lousy country for anyone."

"Why do you stay then?"

Vance spread his hands. "What's a man to do?"

West did not know the answer. Suddenly he was a little sorry for Vance. He felt older than Vance, aged by his wider experience. And then he thought of something else.

"I didn't ask down there, but what is Ma cooking up with Doc Condon?"

Vance's face changed, grew sullen, making him seem more like an Indian than ever. "I taught you never to ask questions when you were a kid. Maybe you forgot it back East, but in these hills people mind their own business."

Without another word he dropped over the rim, disappearing as if the earth had swallowed him.

chapter 8

All the way back to town West puzzled about Condon's visit to the Bentons. He kept telling himself that Vance was right, that it was none of his business. Certainly he had enough trouble of his own without searching for more. But he could not get it out of his mind. Nor could he forget that Ma Benton apparently knew who he was.

It had never occurred to him that the Bentons knew his identity. He had assumed that he was a foundling, picked up perhaps from some ambushed wagon train. Such things had been all too common in the Territory twenty-five years before.

But now the knowledge that if she chose Ma Benton could tell him who he was added a chafing irritation to his already uneasy thoughts. Somehow, some way he would make the old woman tell him.

He rode into town, using the alley to reach the livery, turning the bay into the outer corral, leaving the saddle and bridle on the fence and walking through the runway past the open door of Wentworth's office.

The man waved, but West did not pause. He stepped out onto Railroad Avenue, but before he had traveled halfway to the hotel he heard someone call his name. Turning, he saw Andy Lawrence running toward him across the station yard. He came up, panting, saying as he arrived, "Omstead wants to talk to you. He sent me looking for you an hour ago."

"Who's Omstead?"

"The super, and you'd better talk to him quick. That Dutchy doctor at the hospital was in there, and he's got his knife out for you."

West was surprised. "Gruber? Why should he have his knife out for me?"

"He's scared," Andy said with quick wisdom. "He's afraid you'll get his job. He's a fake."

"What makes you say that?"

"I heard Doc Condon say it. Doc Condon says he wouldn't let Gruber doctor a horse, even if the horse wasn't sick and even if he didn't like the horse."

West grinned. That sounded like Condon after he had been drinking. "Is there anything about this town you don't know, Andy?"

The boy shook his head. "Nope. A fellow's got to know how things are if he's to get ahead."

"How's your mother?"

Andy's eyes glistened. "She's just fine. Laura says she never saw an operation go better. Does it take a lot of practice to learn to operate?"

"It takes a lot of schooling," West said.

Andy was thoughtful. He had never cared particularly for school. He led the way across to the station building and showed West the stairs which led to the offices above. It was very obvious that the boy would like to be present at the interview, but knew the superintendent would not permit it. He stood at the bottom of the steps, watching West climb as if he were watching a friend going to his execution.

Clay Omstead was a small man, and a tough one. Now sixty, he had fought his way up through the ranks to head the railroad's desert division, the longest division of any in the huge, interlocking system.

Nor did he like the job before him. He hated to try a man without a hearing, and that perforce was what he was about to do. But it was not only Gruber's complaint which swayed him. He had received twenty complaints that morning from various citizens of the Springs.

He looked at West curiously as he came in. He saw a tall man with a strong thin face and quiet direct eyes, and wondered if someone had not made a mistake.

"You're West?" He never wasted time beating around things.

"I'm West," the doctor said, and watched the man behind the desk.

Omstead was known to his employees as a driver, but a fair one, and he said now, "This is a job that I don't care for, but one that I trust you will understand is impersonal. I've had a number of complaints about your appointment to our local hospital. I understand you were involved in a train robbery some years ago."

"I was." West's voice was quiet, unhurried. "The Chicago office knew all about it when they hired me."

Omstead had not known that. He said slowly, "Your former association with the Bentons makes you a kind of marked man. I'm surprised that the Chicago office assigned you here. It would have been much wiser if you had been sent to some station where you were not known."

"I requested Soda Springs."

Omstead's estimate of this quiet man rose rapidly. For himself he did not like Gruber, and the opinion of the foreign doctor had very little weight with him.

His blunt fingers strayed across the desk,

picked up a pen holder and toyed with it. "I'm in a peculiar position." He was watching the pen holder now, not West. "Actually the hospital staffs are not directly under the operating department. They are hired and paid directly from Chicago. I have no authority to ask for your transfer, even if I desired to do so. You are under Gruber directly, and Gruber has made it plain that he does not care for your services."

He stopped as if expecting West to comment. The doctor remained silent.

Omstead sighed. This was one of the situations which he disliked thoroughly, a clash of personalities among employees. "All I can say is that if I were you, faced with this kind of a situation, I'd ask for a transfer."

"I doubt it."

Omstead's head jerked up with surprise. "Doubt what?"

West was smiling faintly. "Doubt that you would ask for a transfer. You're a fighter, I think, and stubborn. I suspect you wouldn't want to be run out of a town any more than I do."

Omstead matched his grin. "I think," he said, "that maybe you'll be a match for Gruber at that." He stood up, offering his hand. "Good luck."

West took the hand. Omstead was the

first person who had actually wished him success since he had returned to Soda Springs.

Andy was waiting for him at the foot of the stairs. Andy, he realized, had adopted him, and he could expect the boy to be underfoot at almost any time.

Andy was watching his face. "You get fired?"

"Not quite."

The boy sighed his relief. "I didn't know. Never can tell about old Omstead." He fell into step and together they walked to the hotel.

Laura Hall was at Mary Lawrence's bedside in the laundry. She looked up to see West standing at the door, and then spoke to the woman on the bed.

"Here's the doctor now."

He crossed to the bed and smiled down at Mary, at the same time lifting her wrist to check the pulse. "How do you feel?"

"She has some gas pains," Laura told him, "but she's coming along nicely."

He talked to Mary Lawrence a few minutes, then moved away with Laura at his side. She said curiously, "Belle said that you went to see your outlaw family. Were they glad to see you?"

He shrugged.

"And how long are you going to stay in this horrible town?"

To his surprise he found himself defending Soda Springs. "It's no worse than any other town. All of them have faults."

She was pouting a little. "And what about me? You were a fool to ever come back here. Even your little country girl knows that."

"I told you Belle isn't my girl."

"She's in love with you," Laura said. "I have a good notion to go back East and leave you two stuck with each other."

He was suddenly angry. "Does that mean you don't want to marry me?"

Laura Hall never quarreled with any man except on her own terms. "We'll not talk about it now," she said. "If we do we'll both say something we don't mean." She walked away before he could answer. She usually managed to have the last word.

chapter 9

The Bentons were planning to wreck a train. They planned it as calmly and cold-bloodedly as if they were considering the building of a new fence.

The discussion had started as soon as Doc Condon rode away, for once an idea found its way into Ma Benton's mind she never rested until it was acted upon.

"Doc says that we'll have to have money to take Prince and Duke into Mexico."

They stared at her. They were all standing on the porch of the ranch house. Vance didn't say anything. They all knew that Vance was not in favor of the prison break. Vance did not think it could be done.

Fred asked, "How much money?"

The old lady did not know. "A lot," she said. "We'll want to buy a ranch or something down there."

They considered. They had never earned more than a few dollars honestly in their whole lives. "Condon will have to think up a job for us," Bo said.

His mother shook her head. "I don't trust

Condon now. Since we're putting pressure on him he might just set up a trap for us. What's wrong with planning a job ourselves?"

They looked at each other. Vance said, "You fools. Haven't we got trouble enough? You want to get Duke and Prince out of prison, not join them."

Bo said angrily, "I don't like the way you've been acting."

"Don't like it then." Vance stepped off the porch and walked to the corral. They watched in silence as he caught up his horse and rode out through the canyon.

Fred said, "I just don't understand Vance. Sometimes he don't act like a Benton at all."

"Hell with him," Bo said. "We can get the Dovell boys and Hale and the Armstrongs. That's all we need."

"But what are we going to do?"

Bo said thoughtfully, "The Eastern Express always carries a heavy mail shipment, Eastern banks sending funds to the West Coast. We could stop it at Desert Center."

Fred said, "How are you going to stop it? The Express rolls through there like a bat from hell."

Bo grinned. "The mixed freight always pulls off on the switch to let it pass. Suppose we fixed it so the freight wasn't quite clear of the main line?"

Both Fred and Ma Benton peered quizzically at him.

"That would stop the Express," Bo said. "Chances are the engine crew and the men on the express car would get killed, and the rest would be too shook up to bother us."

"When?" Fred asked.

"What's the matter with tomorrow morning?"

They eyed him for a long moment in silence. Fred started toward the corral. "Let's ride over and talk to the Dovells," he said.

Their mother watched them go, then walked back into the house. She was smiling to herself. Things were beginning to move. One day, not too far away, Duke and Prince would be free.

Fred and Bo rode directly through the hills to the Dovell ranch where they talked to old Ab and his two sons. Then they crossed the ridge and dropped down into White Feather Valley where the Armstrongs had their place.

It was arranged that the Dovell boys and the Armstrongs would meet them at Desert Center with pack horses, and mounts for Bo and Fred. Afterward the Bentons rode on to Soda Springs.

They reached town late in the afternoon and without asking permission hid their horses in Condon's barn. Then they loitered about, trying not to attract attention.

It was their plan to ride the mixed freight when it left the Springs after midnight, staying concealed until it pulled into Desert Center shortly before daylight. They would then overcome the freight crew and leave enough of the freight on the main track to cause the wreck. The plan was as simple as it was brutal.

From a room in one of the cheap hotels across from the station they watched the people on Railroad Avenue. Just before six Bo gave a sudden grunt.

"What's the matter?" Fred asked.

Bo pointed, and Fred saw Hy West come along the street, cross it and head for the Railroad Hospital.

"We're taking him with us tonight," Bo said.

Fred gaped at his brother. "Have you gone crazy?"

Bo shook his head. "It's a chance to get him out of this town without us killing him. Maybe he'll be wiped out in the wreck. We'll stick him in one of the front cars. If not, I'll take care of him then."

Fred didn't like it but he had to agree. He

had no real feeling about West, but he knew how Bo felt about Belle, and when Bo got that Indian look there was no arguing with him.

They timed their invasion of the hospital well. They waited until nearly eleven, then slipped across through the station yard and came up to the platform. Chance played into their hands, for just as they were creeping toward the small building, West stepped out for a smoke.

He stood there, watching as the puffing switch engine busily made up the freight, and did not sense that he was not alone until Fred shoved the gun against his back.

Bo searched him for a weapon and found none. West studied Bo with care as he stepped back. He knew these boys. Neither had much more judgment than a ten-year-old.

"What's this?"

"You're taking a train ride." Bo had been drinking, but he was not drunk. "We're giving you a nice free ride."

Fred said to his brother, "Where's his tools? We'd better send his tools with him. No one would believe a doctor would leave without his tools."

Bo looked at West. "Where are they?"

West decided that they did not mean to

kill him, at least not there, and said, "In the office." He was waiting for a chance to grab the spare gun from Fred's belt. Bo brought out his bag and led him across the welter of tracks. He stopped beside an empty box car close to the head of the train.

Fred took the bag from Bo. He tossed it into the open door of the car. As he did so, West grabbed his extended arm. He swung Fred around, between himself and Bo, at the same time trying to jerk Fred's gun free.

But Fred was like an eel in his grasp. He needed both hands to hold him, and Fred didn't content himself with struggling. He let his legs go slack so that all his weight hung on West's arms, bending him a little forward.

That was all Bo needed. He reached across his brother's shoulder and brought the long barrel of his gun down across West's head in a slashing blow.

West collapsed, falling forward with Fred under him. Bo stooped, dragged his inert body from Fred, then helped his brother to his feet.

"Okay?"

Fred nodded. Together they heaved the unconscious West into the car and rolled the door shut. They crept forward and found places for themselves directly behind the tender. Everything was going on schedule and Bo was happy. Whatever else happened, he felt that he did not need to worry about West again.

chapter 10

West returned to full consciousness slowly. He was at first puzzled by the jolting of the train; then he remembered the Bentons and how he had gotten there. He had no idea how long he had been unconscious, but gray light was filtering in through the crack beside the almost closed door. Dawn came early at this time of year, but it still must be at least four o'clock.

He lay, not caring. The motion of the train jolted him on the hardness of the splintered floor. There was a little hay in the bottom of the car, but not enough to make a real cushion for his aching body.

He lay there a long time and finally realized through his half stupor that the train had stopped. He considered this and found it puzzling. He dragged himself upright then and on rubber legs moved toward the door.

His instrument bag lay where Fred had thrown it. He opened the bag and searched until he found the pills he wanted. Afterward he moved to the door and peered out at the sweep of desert land beyond. They were not in a railroad yard; that much was plain.

It was, he guessed, some lonely siding, and this was confirmed in his mind a moment later by the distant hum of an approaching train.

He was thirsty, and the lump across the top of his head ached dully, and he felt a little tender in the pit of his stomach. The rumble of the on-coming train grew louder, and the loose ground on which the track was built trembled from the vibration of the wheels pounding toward them.

He sat, waiting for the train to pass — and then came an impact which rolled him from his sitting position and sent his body almost to the far end of the car.

There was a grinding crash, like nothing he had ever before experienced. The car jiggled like a bucking horse and slowly rose, tilting as the freight train tried to telescope under the thrusting motion of the driving express. Then it buckled as the coupling broke, and the car seemed for a teetering instant to stand upon its end before it fell sidewise to the desert beyond the right-of-way.

West was battered and bruised. He lay for a moment utterly quiet, and after the smashing, grinding noise the world was suddenly as silent as a tomb. His mind had lost its capacity to judge time. Time was endless. It seemed that the splintering collision had lasted for hours, and afterward the period of silence was endless.

But finally the screaming began.

It brought him to full consciousness as nothing else could have. The car about him was a crumpled thing, twisted out of any recognizable shape.

He lay there, a timber across him, pinning him down, holding him in place yet not hurting him. He had time to wonder about this even as he struggled to free himself. The screams continued. And then he smelled it: a touch of smoke which drifted back through the broken car sides. He smelled it, and he heard the crackle of the flames, and now above the screams he heard the shouts of the rescue workers.

The flames ate their way into his vision, running along the dry wood, aided and nourished by a steady breath of desert wind, growing as they inched along, a wall of fire which seemed to be closing down upon him, licking at him like the forked tongues of a million angry snakes, tightening until he knew that there was no escape. He called. He never knew what he said. He did not hear the shots from without as the Bentons with their friends dragged the sacked mail from the express car and threw it onto the pack horses.

But those shots kept help from coming because they held the crew of the passenger train at bay. The freight crew, those who still lived, were locked in the caboose.

chapter 11

Vance Benton did not know exactly what his brothers' plans were, and he did not want to know — at first. But as he rode away from the ranch, something prompted him to circle back by the hill trail to the rim, where he could watch their actions. Then he had followed them across the hills, first to the Dovell and then to the Armstrong ranch, and afterward into Soda Springs.

He saw how they hid their horses at Condon's and sought seclusion in the cheap hotel, and he watched the hotel from the entrance to Wentworth's livery.

When they left it, late at night he trailed them across the station yard and from the shadows he saw them load West into the empty box car and then seek places for themselves on the train.

He guessed now what they planned to do, and swore under his breath. In his eyes they were fools who could bring nothing but trouble to the family. But the clan feeling remained strong in him, and he almost went to join them.

Instead he went back to Callahan's. He wanted to be certain that he would be seen, that his presence in town would be remembered. He sat in one of the poker games, and stayed with it until after daylight, winning over a hundred dollars, thus establishing his alibi.

Afterward he ate breakfast in the railroad lunchroom and went to Wentworth's livery where he had left his horse.

But instead of saddling the animal and riding out, he loafed in the sun, not quite knowing what to do.

He saw her coming along the sidewalk and knew at once that this must be the girl who had followed Hy West from Chicago. Her clothes were different, and her pink and white face showed no marks of the sun, and her hair was worn differently. To Vance Benton she seemed the prettiest girl in the world.

She passed him in the entrance, lowering her eyes, but not until she had looked into his for one deliberate moment. Then she spoke to Wentworth who stood in the office door.

"I'm looking for Dr. West. He isn't at the hospital and I thought he might have ridden out somewhere. Did he rent a horse from you?"

Wentworth wagged his old head. "He took a horse yesterday, but he brought it back and I haven't seen him since." He called to Vance: "You seen Hy this morning?"

Vance said, "Nope," and as the girl turned to look at him he came forward. "I'm Vance Benton, Miss. You must be the girl Hy was telling me about. The one he's going to marry."

Laura Hall gazed fascinated at Benton. So this was one of the outlaws she had been hearing about. Funny. In her mind she had built up a picture of bearded men in shabby clothes.

Vance was young, not more than a year or two older than West. He was as tall as West, and in some ways more handsome. His thin face had darkened under the desert sun, and his eyes were black and proud. He stared at her with a boldness she found disconcerting, but she rallied to say:

"And you must be the outlaw he was raised with. The one he told me about."

At the word outlaw, Wentworth glanced sharply at Vance. It was one thing to refer to the Bentons as outlaws when they were not present, but quite another to use the word to their faces. In their own way the Bentons considered themselves average citizens who broke the law because they refused to be bound by the conventions other people had created.

But Vance showed no displeasure at her words. Instead, it seemed to please and amuse him that she had heard of him.

"So the Kid mentioned me to you?"

"He did."

"Well what do you know?" He gazed at her with open admiration. "Shame I didn't meet you first."

"You've met me now," she said, "and I'm glad. After all, you and your brothers are the only family Hy has."

It was a new thought to Vance. While he had never teased the younger boy as Bo had, he still had never thought of West as a member of the Benton clan.

He thought fleetingly of West on the freight train, speeding east. He wondered if he should tell her, and decided against it. He wondered what would happen to her here, with West gone, and found the prospect interesting. Vance Benton had known his share of women, most of them from the dance halls of the Southwest, and he had never considered any of them worth more than a second thought. But he had never met anyone like Laura Hall.

She was pretty, very pretty, but he had

seen other pretty girls. It was her poise which struck him, her self-assured manner. Seemed as if she expected everything and everyone to bend easily to her purpose.

She was like a high-strung horse, proud and willful, and the thought crossed his mind that it might be fun to break her.

They stood there for a long moment, appraising each other, trying to guess the strength and weaknesses that the other might have hidden.

And it came to Laura that the man before her was dangerous. She had not found most men dangerous; in fact, her relationships had been highlighted by her own aggressiveness. But some instinct warned her that Vance Benton was different, that anyone who in any way associated with Benton would follow a pattern which he set up.

And while she stood there, trying to think of the proper words, the best way to handle this stranger, a whistle shrilled suddenly from the roundhouse, long and piercing, reaching the farthermost corner of the town.

"A wreck." It was Wentworth, and with agility surprising in one of his age he dashed past her, out into the runway and on into the street.

She turned, surprised, and as the whistle

continued its shrill message she followed
the livery man. Vance was at her heels. They
came together into the sunlight in time to
see the dusty length of Railroad Avenue fill
with excited people, all running toward the
yards.

Laura ran too, not because she thought
that the wreck concerned her, but because
she was caught up by the crowd excitement.

Vance ran at her side, and when she stumbled he put a quick hand under her arm to
steady her. He knew, or figured he knew,
what the wreck was about. And as they ran
on he wondered how Hy West's death
would affect her. It might be hard to comfort her, but it sure as hell would be fun to
try.

chapter 12

Pinned under the splintered beam, Hy West watched the leaping flames inch their way closer, and figured that he had only a matter of minutes to live. Surprisingly, the danger had cleared his head, and he found that the pain was almost entirely gone. He did not panic.

From the time he was able to walk he had faced danger of one kind or another with no one to rely on but himself. He was lying half on his side, half on his stomach, with one arm folded under him, the other out-stretched. His legs were extended, one pinned tightly by the broken piece of the car's siding, so that he could get no pur-chase for his knees in an effort to raise him-self.

But he tried. The sense of survival was very strong within him. He lifted on the arm that was crooked under him, trying to bring the other back until he could get a purchase with his elbow.

He was so engrossed with the effort that he did not hear the freight conductor who was running along the shattered train toward where the two engines had merged in a twisted heap of battered metal.

But the man saw him, and stopped, and then tore into the pile of wreckage which held West a prisoner. The freight conductor worked frantically. He managed to lift the bar across West's shoulder. He managed to free the pinned leg. And somehow West dragged himself to his feet.

As he straightened his toe caught the black bag which had been hurled to the end of the shattered car. He stooped to pick it up and raced after the running man.

They both stopped as they got their first clear view of the wreck and he heard the man beside him sob. "The murderers. The damn murderers."

West turned to look at him. "What are you talking about?"

"The murderers. The two men who locked us in the crummy and left the freight engine sticking out on the main."

A cold feeling like a ball of ice settled at the pit of West's stomach. He steadied himself as he said in a strange voice, "Who were they, where are they now?"

The freight conductor seemed dazed, as if he were suffering from shock. "I don't know. They were masked. They broke out

134

the registered mail and the express and rode away. Someone must have met them here with horses."

He ran on then, with West after him. The Express had been traveling at better than fifty miles an hour and the mail coach and express car and the first pullmans were a twisted jumble of burning wood.

Already the passenger crew was laboring to put out the fire, and one of them had climbed a pole with a jumper instrument to tap the telegraph and send the news of the wreck to the division point.

Both engine crews were dead. Eight passengers were dead and most of the rest injured. West had no clear memory of the next three hours. He worked with the others, halting the fire, prying the injured from the broken cars. Looking at the twisted train it seemed impossible that anyone would have survived, but most had, and the children had fared the best. Not one child was seriously injured.

West worked as he had never worked in his life, spreading blankets on the ground and caring for the victims as they were brought to him.

He was hardly conscious of the arrival of the wrecking train, of Omstead taking charge, of Gruber, red-eyed from his night with the bottle. But Gruber had brought medicine and morphine and he worked at West's side without comment.

Omstead was everywhere. He listened to the reports on the masked men who had raided the mail car, and himself climbed the pole to wire the news to the sheriffs up and down the line.

Already men were tearing up the switch track, using the ties and rails to build a shoofly around the wreck. The crane dumped the broken box cars from the right-of-way, and before darkness came the line was open again for through traffic.

But West knew nothing of this. He worked savagely, endlessly. Gruber was not too much help and West ignored him. When the special came he supervised the removal of the injured to the hospital at Soda Springs.

One woman died during the ride, four more were borderline, the rest had varying injuries from broken bones to black eyes. Omstead had noticed West when he first arrived, but not until late afternoon did he find time to ask the freight conductor how West happened to be there.

The man shrugged. "He was in one of the box cars, beating his way I guess. I hauled him out and was damn glad to find he was a doctor. Who is he?"

Omstead did not bother to answer. He had other things to trouble him. For one thing he had just learned that Andy and Sam Dillon had managed to stow themselves away in one of the toilets of the special, and had escaped the brakeman until they arrived at the scene of the wreck.

The boys immediately attached themselves to West. He sent them on a hundred errands while preparing to load the more seriously injured aboard the special. Afterward, he made room for the walking cases, and not until all of these were safely in place did he permit the uninjured to board the train.

When they arrived at Soda Springs he again brushed Gruber aside, and went about setting up the ward as best he could. He sent Andy and Sam out to find Laura, Belle, and any other town women who would volunteer. When Laura came he put her in charge, avoiding her questions as to where he had been and how he happened to become involved in the wreck.

Soda Springs was a railroad town, and it was affected by the wreck in the same way that a mining village is affected by a disaster underground. The people turned out in mass, and Condon appeared almost at once, offering his services. West accepted gratefully. He had lost all patience with Gruber, and he simply did not have enough hands to do everything that was required. For three days he lived in a kind of nightmare and a number of things happened of which he was only vaguely aware. First was a telegraph order in response to Gruber's protest. West was relieved at Soda Springs and ordered to report to the home office.

Gruber brought the order on the second morning after the wreck. There was whisky on his breath and triumph in his round, brown eyes.

"You can leave today," he told his former assistant. "I'll take over from now on."

West looked around him. There were still twenty-seven patients in the small, over-crowded hospital. The others had been patched up and sent on to the coast.

Three of those remaining would not live. West was certain of that, although he and Condon had done everything they could. Strain, coupled with his anger at Gruber, made his voice sharp.

"You'll get out of here," he said, quietly, "and you'll stay out as long as any of these people remain here."

Gruber started to bluster. In the world from which he had come an underling did not question authority, but West wasted no further words. He walked around the desk, catching the older man by his coat collar and swinging him about. He walked Gruber down the hall and threw him through the door to the platform beyond.

Gruber went to his knees. He started to get up, then saw West still in the doorway, waiting for him to rise. He turned and scuttled away on hands and knees. He had almost reached the corner of the building when Condon rounded it and stopped in surprise. Gruber scrambled to his feet and beat a hasty retreat. Condon stared after him in amazement.

"What's happened to Dutchy now?"

"I threw him out."

For the first time he could remember he saw approval in the old doctor's blood-shot eyes. "Wish I'd gotten here three minutes sooner. Anyway, you'd better go talk to Omstead. I'll take over here."

West nodded and after showing Condon the charts, left the hospital for the first time since bringing the patients from the wreck, and walked toward the station.

Omstead was in his office. He finished dictating an order to a clerk, then swung around to face West as the clerk left. "Been meaning to see you, but I've been so damn busy with the wreck and the holdup."

West had a sudden flash of guilt. He had meant to tell Omstead about the Bentons, but he too had been busy. Now he tried to make amends.

Omstead heard him out, carefully expressionless. "You're sure it was Bo and Fred Benton?"

"Certain. I've known them all my life."

"But you don't know that they had anything to do with the holdup. They might have dumped you on that train and not gotten on themselves?"

West had to admit it was possible. "I'd guess, though, that they rode the train and that Vance met them with some horses."

Omstead frowned. "Then you'd guess wrong. Vance Benton played poker at Callahan's all that night. He was here in town when news of the wreck reached us. Maybe the others were in it, but Vance was not. We've been checking on them all, naturally."

"And what did you find?"

The super shrugged. "Nothing. Bo and Fred claim they were at a dance at one of the hill ranches, someone named Armstrong. Of course the people there may be lying. All those people hang together out there, but we can't prove it." He sounded discouraged. "And I'm afraid your story won't help much. A lot of people in this town are wondering how you happened to be on that train. Several have reminded me that you were mixed up in one holdup, and that merely because you turned to and helped take care of the injured doesn't mean you weren't tied in with the robbers."

West flushed.

"I don't believe it," Omstead told him, "and don't worry about it. By the way, there's a telegraphic order relieving you of duty."

West's flush deepened. "Gruber came to tell me. I threw him out of the office."

Omstead laughed, then sobered. "I don't blame you, and as far as I'm concerned you can stay here as long as you like. But you can't keep Gruber out of his hospital. I'll have a talk with him and try to straighten it out. Now go back and get some rest. You look as if you haven't slept in days."

West went back to the hospital and found that Condon and Laura seemed to have everything under full control. Then he went into his own office and stretched out on the couch. He fell asleep almost at once.

In the ward West had just left, Condon was studying Laura closely. He had to admit that she seemed to be a good nurse, but he did not like women in general and he found that he did not like this girl in particular.

Laura was quick to sense his attitude. She had watched Condon during the days as he helped with the wreck victims, hoping that she could catch him in a slip which she could turn to her own advantage.

She resented him for his apparent hold on West, and she was also a little afraid of him. But her manner when she addressed him was always carefully correct.

She came over to speak to him now, reminding him that they were out of morphine and that none had arrived on the afternoon train.

He nodded, still busy dressing a burn. He pulled the keys to his own medicine closet from his pocket, tossing them to her and telling her how to find his house.

Ordinarily she might have resented being sent on this errand, but this afternoon she was pleased to get away from the hospital. She felt free as she moved up the street, ignoring the stares of the people, until she saw Vance Benton riding toward her.

She told herself that she had no interest in the tall man, that she would be a fool to get mixed up with the Bentons.

But despite this denial her interest did quicken, and she could not resist the impulse to raise her hand in greeting as he rode up.

Vance was never a person to stand on ceremony. All his life his actions had been direct. He had taken what he wanted when he was strong enough to get it, and he had decided during the last few days that he wanted this girl.

He stepped from the horse, looped the reins over the rail and ducked under it to join her on the sidewalk. His clothes as usual were worn but clean, and also he was clean-shaven. Somehow this impressed Laura. She had seen many other riders during her short stay in the Springs, and few of them were either shaven or clean.

He came to her side with the easy, cat-like grace which marked all his movements, and took her arm as if by right, saying in his drawling voice,

"How's my nurse?"

She was very conscious of his nearness, of the touch of his fingers on her arm. This for her was a new experience, this quick awareness, and to her it rang a small bell of warning. She who all through her short life had been the huntress had suddenly become the hunted. It was pleasing to know that a man wanted you, that you had made him want you, and yet be able to stand as one detached, to remain objective about him, even when you were pretending to surrender to him.

But with Vance she sensed that it would not be a case of token surrender. He would take what he wanted at the first opportunity. For once in her life she had met a person stronger and more ruthless than she was.

To mask her unease she made her voice light, saying pertly,

"And how is my pet outlaw?"

His white teeth showed for one instant in his dark, wind-burned face, and then he walked along beside her, indifferent to the interest which his presence caused the shoppers they passed.

Beyond the small tight business section he told her easily, "Your reputation in the Springs is ruined for all time. You were seen on the streets with a Benton. What are you doing up this way?"

"Morphine," she said, and explained that Condon had sent her to his office.

Vance swore under his breath. "The old fool, sending you up here to face those mongrel dogs."

"I'm not afraid of dogs."

There was open admiration in his eyes. "I don't believe you're afraid of much of anything. Another girl would be afraid of me."

She knew better than to ask, but she could not resist. "And why should I be afraid of you?"

He grinned down at her. "You know the answer to that one. A man sees a woman, what does he want?"

She knew that she should stop this conversation, but she found herself saying, "That depends upon the man, and the girl."

Suddenly he was gravely serious. "I'm talking about us, Laura. We're different from ordinary people. We take what we want."

"Do we?" She knew that her voice was not quite steady. Damn him. What right did he have to make her feel this way?

"We do," Vance said, and then stopped. They had reached Condon's gate and the dogs came charging out, leaping high against the firm planks.

In spite of herself Laura flinched, and Vance laughed at her. "Not so bold now."

She said, "Those horrible animals. They sound as if they would tear me apart."

"You're all right with me," he told her. "They know me. I've been here a lot."

She found a moment to wonder why Vance should have spent much time with the old doctor. Then he opened the gate and began kicking the cringing dogs out of their path, cursing them as he did so.

The animals fell back, disappearing around the corner of the house, cowed by his presence. Vance led her up the path and pushed open the door.

As she stepped in she peered curiously around the untidy, dirty room. Her hatred of Condon sharpened her interest as she noted the cluttered table, the old desk and the medicine cabinet.

She unlocked the cabinet's battered door and found the morphine. She relocked the cabinet and turned. And as she turned, she saw the tintype above the desk.

The beauty of the face astonished her. She wondered who the woman was, wondered how anyone so lovely could have had anything to do with the monstrosity which Condon had become. She sensed a story here, and she nodded at the picture.

"Do you know who that is?"

Vance said without interest, "Someone the old doc really hates, I guess. I've seen him stand and curse her for half an hour when he's drunk, but when I asked him once he told me to mind my own damn business."

Laura continued to study the picture, and she noted the photographer's name and Philadelphia address on the frame.

Abruptly she obeyed an impulse. She let Vance lead her out to the sun-baked yard, then muttered an excuse and ducked back into the room.

When she rejoined Vance the picture was safely concealed beneath her dress, and for some reason she felt gayer than she had in days.

"Vance," she said, "do me a favor and take this morphine over to Condon. I want to go on to the hotel and get some breakfast."

He accepted the medicine and the key. "When am I going to see you?"

"I don't know."

"Go riding with me tonight."

She pretended embarrassment. "You know I can't do that. I'm engaged to Hy West."

He caught her arm roughly and swung her around. For an instant she was afraid that he was going to kiss her there on the street, and knew suddenly with a feeling of weakness that she wanted the feel of his mouth, hard against her own.

"Stop playing with me." There was a savagery in his voice she had never heard before. "Meet me behind the livery at eight."

"And if I don't?"

He held her by both arms, so close that she could feel his warm breath against her cheek. "If you don't I'll come and drag you out, no matter where you are."

He was gone then, releasing her as suddenly as he had grabbed her, striding away, cutting directly across the wide street to the hospital building without looking back.

For an instant she stood helpless, her knees so weak that she feared to move. Then slowly she walked on toward the hotel, knowing as she went that whatever happened she did not dare meet Vance Benton that night.

But at eight o'clock she found him in the deep shadow, near the corral, standing beside two saddled horses. Neither spoke, neither made a sound as he lifted her into the saddle and then mounted his own animal. He led them out, circling the town by a little used path.

To the right were the far-flung lights of the railroad yard. Ahead to the east were the fainter lights of the fort three miles away. Above them a million stars turned the dark arch of the sky to a milky hue.

Laura never knew how far they rode. She only knew that finally Vance pulled his horse from the trail and they followed a small, side canyon, the matted grass deadening the sound of their horses.

Then they dismounted and the gurgle of the stream sounded somewhere to the right, and the trees above them made a ragged outline against the sky, and suddenly Vance's arms were about her, his teeth hard, pressing against her lips.

She had never known anything quite like this. The innate savagery of the man stunned her. She felt that she should fight him, but her desires stopped her.

They were on the grass now, and she experienced something which she had never before known, that she had believed did not actually exist. Her body came alive for him as it never had for anyone else. It was as if it moved of its own volition, without control or direction from her mind.

She was crying softly, her fingernails digging into his bare shoulders as if to hold him to her always. Afterward they did not talk. They lay quiet for a long time, and then slowly, reluctantly, they rose and went back to their horses.

Belle saw them ride up to the rear door of the hotel. Belle was not trying to spy. Belle had come into the kitchen to get a glass of water for Mary Lawrence.

She heard their horses in the alley and was surprised. She looked out in time to see

149

Vance help Laura from the saddle. She watched them kiss for a long moment before she turned away.

But she could not get out of the kitchen before Laura came in. Laura stopped, just inside the door.

"So you've been watching for me," Laura said. "Well, I hope it does you as much good as you think it will."

She stalked past Belle, went through the dining room and up the stairs.

chapter 13

Hy West knew nothing of Laura's ride with Vance Benton. Laura did not tell him, and Belle did not mention it, and he was much too busy trying to save the injured. He hardly left the hospital. He slept on a cot in his office and took his meals in the kitchen.

Gruber had come back, but by Omstead's orders he left West strictly alone. Omstead had wired Chicago that he could not spare West. He got no reply, and then the pox struck, and he along with the others forgot all about it.

It was Gruber who discovered the pox. He came into West's office to find Laura Hall and West checking supplies which had arrived on the morning train.

West looked up as Gruber came in, expecting some kind of argument. It seemed that he and Gruber did nothing but argue whenever they met.

But Gruber was too tense with excitement to remember his differences with the younger doctor.

"It's the smallpox," he half shouted. "The

smallpox. I am not mistaken. I tell you I know the smallpox when I see it."

West took three quick steps forward and grabbed Gruber's arm.

"Keep your voice down. What are you talking about? Who has the smallpox?"

Gruber tried to shake free. "The man in the bed at the end of the ward. The one who lost a hand in the wreck."

"When did you find this out? Who already knows?"

Gruber wet his lips. "Condon and one of the volunteer nurses. She ran away as soon as I told them what it was."

West swore under his breath. "The news will be all over town in fifteen minutes."

He was wrong. It was all over town within ten minutes, and Soda Springs reacted with quick fear. The frontier dreaded no scourge more than the pox.

West made his plans swiftly, but he knew that whatever they did they were still in for trouble. At least fifty of the townspeople had been in and out of the hospital within the last few days.

"We'll have to vaccinate everyone who's been exposed," he said.

Gruber was gloomy. "In Europe you can force vaccination, but here — there is no law."

West said grimly, "We'll vaccinate them, law or no law."

"Have you sufficient lymph?" Laura Hall had recovered her composure and as always, was being practical.

"I'll wire for more. In the meantime we'll set up a quarantine of the hospital, and arrange for a pest house for anyone who contracts the pox."

"Where?"

He thought quickly. "In the baggage shed. Have one of the porters clear it out and clean the floor." But when he went to inspect the work an hour later he found that nothing had been done. The porters had vanished, fearful of infection. The volunteer workers who had helped so unselfishly with the wreck victims had disappeared. Even Condon had walked out, explaining that his private practice had to be cared for. West found himself with the whole hospital to run and no one to help him but Gruber and Laura Hall.

There were two more cases by the following morning, and he could only conclude that someone from the wrecked train must have carried the infection, perhaps someone who died during the accident without anyone knowing that he had been sick.

The next week became a nightmare, not only for West but for the whole southern end of the Territory. Fear like a racing forest fire spread across the whole of the thinly populated land. Two cases had broken out among the volunteer nurses who had helped at the hospital. The supplies arrived from Chicago and West sent out a call for the Soda Springs citizens to come in and be vaccinated.

Only a few came. He appealed first to the sheriff and then to the town marshal for help. Instead of assisting they ignored his plea and set up a quarantine law of their own, manned by volunteers to keep anyone from the hospital from crossing Railroad Avenue.

West learned of this line from Belle Callahan, who had volunteered on the second day and was assisting with both the nursing and the cooking. She came into his office from the hospital kitchen, her face flushed, her eyes angry.

"That Bruce Gimble!"

West was very tired. He had been on duty for twenty-four hours without sleep, and one of his patients had died at daybreak.

"What's Gimble done now?"

"You know that man who died this morning. Well, we had two of the Mexican section hands — boys who had already had the pox — put the body in a coffin and take it out for burial."

He nodded.

"Gimble and his men drove them back. They say no one from railroad property is allowed to go uptown."

West's mouth tightened.

"And they're telling everyone that you are purposely spreading the plague."

He blinked at her, startled. "Spreading it?"

"That's right. Gimble made a speech. I heard him. He said you'd always been a cold-blooded killer at heart, and everyone in town knows you should have gone to prison, and you know how they feel and you hate the town because of it, and you'd be perfectly happy to see everyone in Soda Springs die —"

"Surely no one is fool enough to believe that!"

"People," Belle Callahan said, "are fools enough to believe anything when they're afraid. And they're afraid now. They look at everyone they meet on the streets, wondering who's carrying germs and who isn't. A good third of the population has already pulled out for the hills."

"The best thing they could do," West said

slowly. "If they won't be vaccinated, the farther away they can keep from each other the better."

"And there are four new cases in town. They won't bring them here. They've set up their own pest house out at McClune's ranch. They've got some men who have already had the pox caring for them, and Condon is advising them on the proper treatment."

"So much the better. It leaves less for us to handle."

They were interrupted by the opening door. West saw Andy Lawrence standing in the entrance. The boy had been one of the few in town to submit to vaccination, but still West did not want him at the hospital.

"Son, you know better than to come in here."

Andy was almost crying with excitement. "I had to come. I had to warn you. They're fixing it up to hang you."

"Hang me?" West swung about. "What are you talking about?"

"Bruce Gimble. He's got ten men who've had the pox. They've volunteered to come in here, and they're going to move all the sick people on a train and send them away, and then they are going to hang you, and afterwards they're going to burn the railroad

156

buildings. They think that burning the buildings will kill the germs."

West started for the door. "I've got to warn Omstead."

"They've already got Omstead." Andy was barring his progress. "And the ticket agent and the master mechanic and Boone Grantline. They've taken them to the far end of the yards, and they're forcing them to make up a train, and when the train is ready they're coming here."

Belle Callahan's face was very white. "You'd better slip out the back door, Hy. I'll get my father. Surely there must be someone left in town who hasn't completely lost his mind."

"No use," Andy said. "They've got their quarantine line all around. They let me through because they didn't see these, but they won't let anyone out." He pulled open his coat and showed his father's gunbelts underneath.

"I brought you these, Hy."

West reached out and helped the boy unfasten the heavy belts. For the barest instant he hesitated, feeling Belle's eyes upon him. Then deliberately he fastened the belts in place, lifting first one gun and then the other, making certain that they were loaded.

Afterward he said, "Both of you stay in

here. Don't come out no matter what happens," and went quickly through the office door into the hall. He passed Gruber just inside the entrance and from the man's white face judged that he already knew about the mob in the lower yards.

He had a momentary flash of contempt for the man's obvious fear, and then he stepped out onto the sunlit wooden platform.

From where he stood he could see them working at the train, three cars behind the switch engine. And as he took his place he saw it move slowly, backing toward the station with the mob walking beside it.

He glanced to his left, out at Railroad Avenue, and saw the thin line of men spread along the opposite sidewalk at the far side of the wide street. Andy had not been exaggerating. The railroad property was completely surrounded, with the hospital at the center of an irregular circle.

He stepped back a little, so that the hospital corner was between him and the street, and stood facing down the yards. He watched the makeshift train back slowly toward him, watched the mob close ranks behind Gimble and come on, heading for the spot at which he stood.

He was not afraid for himself. He did not

believe they would hang him although mob psychology was a peculiar thing, and undoubtedly some of them had been drinking. The hanging talk had only been Gimble's way of stirring them up. But he had no intention of letting them load the sick on that train. Such an action would result in several deaths.

They had seen him. Gimble pointed, and they increased their speed. They had seen him, but they had not yet seen the heavy gunbelts crossed at his waist.

They came on, and he knew by the way they moved that his guess had been correct. Gimble had fired their courage with alcohol. Alcohol and fear: it was a bad combination. Men had done many foolish things in the grip of alcohol and fear.

He watched them, feeling set apart, as he had so often felt when he was a boy, set apart and rejected. But for some reason he no longer hated them. Instead he felt a very deep contempt for the mob which was following Gimble so blindly.

They were closer now, and he saw their flushed faces distinctly. There were six men behind Gimble, the rest halting as the train stopped beside the station. And still he waited until they stepped up from the tracks to the platform, hardly ten feet from where he stood. He spoke then to Gimble and at the same time opened the white coat so they could not miss the fact that he was wearing Dave Lawrence's guns.

"That's far enough, Marshal."

Gimble stopped, one foot raised, his eyes surprised as they fastened on the guns sagging at West's hips. Ever since the doctor's return to the Springs, Gimble had observed West closely, and this was the first time that he had seen the doctor armed.

He had not expected it, and the knowledge came as a shock. He had never seen West shoot as a boy, but there had been wild stories of his ability during the trial following the holdup, and Gimble was by nature a cautious man.

The men behind him surged on, pushing him forward until he was forced to use his elbows to hold them back.

"Wait a minute."

A bearded man whom West did not recognize seemed not to be impressed. His liquor-slurred words carried clearly along the platform. "What's the matter? Let's get him."

West said mockingly, "Is that your idea, Gimble — to get me?"

The marshal was sweating. It had seemed so very easy when they planned this move in

Callahan's bar. All they needed to do was to seize the station and the roundhouse, force the railroad employees to make up a special train, load up the sick people from the hospital and send them down the line.

He had spoken of hanging West. He had done that merely to inflame his audience. He didn't really care what happened to the doctor.

But he had not expected any opposition once they had control of the station, and it angered him now that they should be so close to their objective and yet be blocked by one man.

He controlled himself with an effort, managing to say in a fairly normal tone, "We want no more trouble than is necessary. Keep out of this while we load the train. You can ride with your sick if you like. We don't care what happens then, but this town does not want the plague."

"No one wants the plague." West's voice was low, but it had a carrying quality which reached them all. "But you are not moving anyone this morning. These people stay where they are, and they stay until they have recovered completely."

Gimble almost lost control, then. His voice cracked from sheer nervousness. "Don't be a fool. Look around. We have fifty armed men at least."

"You can have a hundred." West still spoke in that calm voice. "You can't move these people."

Gimble's face contorted. "I'm giving you one last chance. Stand aside while we load them."

"No, Gimble. No other town wants the pox. If we move them we chance further infection. I'll kill you if you try to move them. I'll kill as many as I can of those with you, but I'll kill you first."

For a moment no one stirred. He watched them all, but mostly Gimble, seeing the sudden raw desire in Gimble's eyes. Gimble was trying to steel himself to the point where he would reach for the gun at his hip. Gimble had killed three men in the line of duty.

West watched his eyes. He saw the purpose grow. He saw the man's fingers spread and then fan down suddenly toward the butt of his single weapon.

West's hands dropped. He pulled both guns, just as Gimble got his free of the holster. West fired, his bullet tearing the gun from Gimble's grasp, spinning it away. A smear of blood grew on the marshal's finger.

Gimble stared down at it stupidly, not realizing for an instant what had happened.

Then reaction set in and he started to shake.

West had fired only one gun, the right one, and fired but once. The other gun covered the men behind the marshal. None of them had moved. They stood like so many leaderless sheep, uncertain and afraid.

West knew a crowd, and he knew that there were moments when you could sway them and moments when you would fail.

"Had enough?" His words were thrown at the marshal, but they included the men behind him.

And Gimble broke. With a muttered curse he turned and headed for Railroad Avenue, clutching his injured wrist. The men who had followed him only minutes before hesitated, staring at the lone figure before them, at the big guns still steady in his hands.

They still wanted the plague sufferers driven out of town. They hated the quiet man before them and would have hanged him had they dared, but their cohesion was gone. They were no longer a mob, following blindly, given a feeling of security by their numbers. They were individuals, threatened by the guns in the hands of a man who had shown that he was both able and willing to use them.

Suddenly they too broke, hurrying off as if

each dreaded to be the last one on that platform. West watched them go, but he did not budge. Where he stood he was screened from the men patrolling the far side of Railroad Avenue, but if he were to step forward he would be exposed to their fire and might easily lose the victory he had just won.

He held his place, calling to those members of the mob who still guarded the special train. "All right, boys. Get off railroad property and stay off."

They hesitated. They might well have shot at him, but they had seen Gimble go and the men with him follow, and they felt deserted. First one edged away, and then the whole crowd dispersed, hurrying now as if they would not feel safe until they had crossed the town's main street.

At once, the railroad crowd they had been holding as prisoners on the train came thronging down the steps, Omstead in the lead, angry now, spoiling for revenge.

Despite his lack of size, Omstead was a born fighter. He had not relished being herded aboard the train at gun point, but he was level-headed enough to realize that this was not the time for a pitched battle between the railroad workers and the town.

He came along the platform extending his hand to West. "This is the second time you've proved yourself," he said as they shook hands. "First at the wreck, now here. I'll tell you now that you can stay in Soda Springs as long as I am running this division. I don't care what Chicago says."

He turned to Boone Grantline who was at his heels. "Wire Kansas City. Tell them to send a dozen railroad police with rifles, men who've been vaccinated or have had the pox. If Gimble wants to play rough we'll show him how. In the meantime dig up some guns. Arm the wipers and the switchmen. Throw a guard around the yards and the station and tell them to shoot the first sonofabitch that crosses our lines without permission." He wiped his face with a handkerchief. "That was real fancy shooting, Doc. Did you mean to get his hand or just knock his gun down?"

West gave him a small grin. "I meant to hit him in the belly. I guess I'm kind of out of practice."

Omstead could not decide whether to believe him or not.

chapter 14

Dr. Albert Condon had no love for his fellow men and in a way he found himself amused by the reaction of Soda Springs to the threat of the plague.

Nor was the gripping fear confined to the town. The whole southern half of the Territory lay in its grasp and every settlement looked on each newcomer with sharp suspicion.

But it was not until Condon received the wire from the doctor at the Territorial Prison that he sensed the scope of the terror which embraced the countryside. The wire told Condon that one of the inmates had developed suspicious symptoms and in panic asked if Condon could cooperate in vaccinating all the prisoners. It was then that the solution to his problem flashed into Condon's mind.

Condon answered the call as he had answered the others in the past, for the prison doctor was entirely incapable and often summoned Condon's aid. He rode the thirty intervening miles in the local's smoker, as the only passenger in the dirty car. People were not exposing themselves to the possibility of infection unless absolutely necessary.

Condon sat gazing through the clouded window at the broken hills which stretched away southward toward the border, and tried to complete his plan. Once or twice he almost discarded it as unworkable, but after he reached the prison and saw the terror with which the officials viewed the possibility that the plague might break out within the walls, he decided to go ahead with it.

The prisoner had the pox; there could be no doubt about it. Condon had him isolated, promised to send for lymph in sufficient quantity to vaccinate the others, and returned to Soda Springs. Less than an hour after he arrived at the yellow station he was on his horse, heading for the Benton ranch.

He had not expected a warm reception, but was totally unprepared for the welcome that he got. Before he could step down from his horse beside the corral fence, both Bo and his mother appeared from the house, and Bo was carrying a rifle.

"That's far enough, Doc."

Condon dismounted, ignoring the rifle, and walked toward them. "What in hell's the matter with you now?"

167

"The plague," Ma said. "We don't want it here."

Condon swore, but kept walking. "I hope you all get it and die of it," he told them. "Put that damn gun down. The plague in this part of the country is about over. Why in the devil didn't you come in and be vaccinated?"

They looked at him uncertainly. Bo said slowly, "What brings you out here anyway?"

"I promised to think of a way to free Duke and Prince."

Nothing else could have driven the fear of the sickness so quickly from the old woman's mind.

"You've got a plan?" she said.

He nodded, and she said, "Come up to the porch but don't step inside. The germs might be on your clothes."

Condon didn't argue. For the first time in weeks he was thoroughly enjoying himself. His thinking had always had a sardonic quality. He enjoyed the mechanics of plotting, the feeling that he was sitting behind the scenes and motivating the actions of others as if they were puppets controlled by strings.

He wasted no time. He explained exactly what had to be done, and why the prison break had a better than average chance of success. "The warden is a fool," he said. "The prison doctor is worse, and they're scared to death of an epidemic within the walls. They know if anything like that happens there will be an investigation of conditions within the prison, and they can't afford that.

"Now our main problem is that both Duke and Prince have been anything but model prisoners. They've spent more time in solitary than they have out, which makes it doubly difficult to get guns in to them.

"But if they could fake being sick they would be removed to quarantine, especially if that dunce of a doctor thinks they might be coming down with the pox. Whenever anything like that happens he always sends for me."

Ma Benton's face lighted. "Then you'll take the guns in to the boys."

Condon swore at her. "I won't. After the break I'd be the first to be suspected if I'd so much as seen them." He let his voice change quickly. "Don't worry, I have it all figured out. They've asked me to help vaccinate the prisoners. I'm sending Pedro Martinez down with the lymph. He's had the pox."

Bo laughed suddenly. "Pedro's the biggest horse thief that ever came out of the breaks."

"And he owes me a favor for saving his boy last year. He'll do what I tell him. Now, here's what you have to do." He was looking at the woman. "You are to go to the prison tomorrow. You are to tell the warden that you haven't much longer to live, that you want to see Duke and Prince once more before you die."

He pulled a small package of white powders from his pocket. "If they search you and find these you can say it's your own medicine. Give these powders to the boys, tell them to take two apiece. It won't kill them but it will make them vomit. They're to wait four days after you've been there before they take the powders, and then they're to complain of headaches and pains in their backs. They're to rub the skin of their foreheads with dust or pebbles or something, close to the hairline so that it's reddened. The doctor will be so sure that it's the pox that he won't be too thorough in his examination."

"Then what?" They were both watching him closely.

"I've sent for lymph from Chicago. The doctor will have isolated Duke and Prince, probably in the old stables. He'll want me to see them, but I'll swear that I haven't the time. However I'll leave Pedro as a nurse. In

170

his bag of medicine he'll have the guns. They'll wait until the following night. You, Bo, get as many riders from the hills as you can trust, and some spare horses. Be in the arroyo behind the prison just after sundown.

"With the guns, Duke and Prince will break into the yard. If they're lucky they'll get out the main gate without too much trouble. Then the lot of you will head for the border, taking Pedro with you. If there's any question about the escape the blame will be on him. He can stay below the line. He has fifty relatives down there."

The pleasure which had been building up in Ma Benton's face died. "That's the only part I don't like. If they could just come home sometime."

"They can never come home," Condon said flatly. "I suppose you've got enough money stashed away from that train wreck." He looked at Bo who met his glance blandly.

Condon said, "That was a damn fool thing to do. The country still thinks you did it. The only thing which has saved you so far is the fact that Vance was in town all that night. They can't understand the Bentons riding without Vance riding with them."

Bo could not understand that either, but

he did not answer. Condon rode away, feeling relieved. If the Bentons succeeded in breaking their brothers out of prison none of them would dare cross the line from Mexico for years.

That was fine with Condon. He was through with the Bentons, no matter what happened. And if the break proved successful, the chances were that most of them would be killed. If any survived they would certainly be fugitives. Either way it was all right with the old doctor, and for the first time in his life he felt that he was growing old. He rode up to his place, dismounted heavily, unsaddled, turned the horse into the little corral and with a sigh of relief headed for the house, ignoring the dogs as they crowded forward for his greeting.

He entered the cluttered front room, tossed his hat to the table, and sat down in the chair before the desk.

He was very tired. It seemed to him that he had scarcely slept since the train wreck, and he had not permitted himself more than a few casual drinks. He bent forward, opened the lower drawer and pulled out a partly filled bottle. As was his wont, he raised the bottle in a sardonic toast to the picture which hung above the desk. His hand paused, shaking. The picture was not there. A lighter square on the soiled wall showed where it had hung.

For a moment he sat motionless, staring at the wall, trying to recall when he had last noticed the picture in place. Had he been drinking through the last few weeks he might believe he had destroyed it in one of his drunken rages. He had been tempted many times during the past years.

But he'd stayed sober. . . . He rose, pulling the desk away from the wall to be sure the picture had not fallen to the floor. Then he searched through the piles of junk which had accumulated in the various corners. The picture was not in the room. Either he had thrown it away, or someone had taken it. His first thought was of West, but he discarded that almost at once. The boy had shown no curiosity regarding the picture, even during the two years he had lived in this house.

Someone must have stolen the picture. But who? How had they gotten past the dogs? It might have been one of the Bentons. He frowned at the thought, then discarded it also. Puzzled, he drank deeply from the bottle. For some reason which was not entirely clear to him the loss of the picture came as a shock. He drank again, and yet again, and afterward he slept in the chair.

chapter 15

Riding home well after midnight, Vance Benton considered his own future. He had never given it a great deal of thought before, but he was not a person who set out deliberately to deceive himself.

The impact of Laura Hall upon him had been far greater than he had expected. At first it had been little more than a game with him. It had amused his bitter sense of humor to attempt to take the girl for no other reason than that she was different from the women he had known and therefore offered a challenge to his vanity.

But as the affair had progressed he found it harder and harder to do without her. Love was something which he hardly understood. His feeling for his family was a clan relationship, a certain responsibility which was not complicated by any other emotion.

But now, amazingly, he was stirred by ambition, by a desire to get away from these hills, a desire to make something of himself.

This stemmed directly from Laura. After that initial ride together she had refused to see him again, but he had met her the following night, and the next and the next.

For the first time in her self-centered existence Laura found it impossible to follow the level dictates of her cautious mind. In Vance's arms everything else faded to nothingness. She was in love. She knew it, and resented it, and fought against it.

But something within her cried out for Vance and she surrendered herself to him again and again although she swore that each time would be the last.

Sobbing in his arms, she lashed out with bitter words as she felt the structure of her carefully planned world slip away from her.

"This is crazy," she had almost shouted. "What do you expect me to do — live in a mountain cabin, away from people, like a coyote skulking in a hole, while you go out and steal a few horses?"

"To hell with that," he'd said roughly, stopping her words by kissing her fiercely. "I'll pull out. We'll go away, away someplace where they have never heard of me. Hy West did it. Why can't I?"

Why couldn't he indeed? His resolve was taken now. He would go away. He had no actual idea of where he would go, or what he would do. At the instant he felt as much in prison as if he had been sharing the cell with Duke and Prince.

He gave no thought to the fact that Laura was supposed to marry West, that there had been no break between them, that West had been too engrossed with his work to learn about his relationship with Laura.

He rode through the canyon mouth into the ranch yard, stepped down and pulled his saddle from the weary animal. Loosing the horse into the corral, he walked toward the house.

Bo had heard him coming. Bo was waiting on the porch. Bo's voice shook a little from his inner excitement. "We're going to get Duke and Prince out of prison."

Vance stopped. He and Bo had hardly spoken since he had refused to help in wrecking the train, and he had been so involved with Laura that he had forgotten all about the possible prison break.

He stared at his younger brother. "How are you going to do it?"

Bo told him, his voice rising with tension as he talked. "I've already lined up a dozen men to ride with us. It's all set. We've got the money from the train wreck hidden and if Condon and the Mexican do their parts it can't fail."

Vance leaned against the post. His tone gave no indication of the despair within him.

"So we head for Mexico." Before his mind rose a picture of the Mexican villages he had seen, the mud and straw huts, the dust, the heat, a backward land filled by a sleepy people. A fine prospect for anyone. Certainly no place to take Laura Hall.

He said, "The whole idea is crazy."

Bo never thought beyond the next move. Bo's voice hardened. "What's happened to you? I believe you're scared."

Vance looked at him squarely. "Yes, I'm scared, but you wouldn't understand what I'm afraid of. I'm afraid of the years ahead, of what that kind of life will do to me, of being cheated of everything I want, of going on and on the way we are now."

"I don't get what you mean." As always when he failed to understand Bo turned sullen.

"I didn't expect you would. You're in love with Belle, aren't you?"

Bo's sullenness increased. "What's that got to do with it?"

"You going away and leave her?"

Bo considered. He began to see what Vance meant. This was the jumping-off place. If they went through with the prison break he would never again ride freely into Soda Springs, never again see this ranch.

"I might take her with me," he said

without conviction.

"Think she'd come?"

Deep in his heart Bo knew that she would not. Even with his exalted ego he could not fully persuade himself that he stood any real chance with Belle Callahan. Until this minute the idea of possessing her had been a nebulous thing, a part of a dream with which he had lulled himself to sleep on more than one lonely night.

"I could make her," he said, his resolve crystallizing. "By God, that's an idea. If I had her down there she'd be damn glad to marry me."

Vance did not answer. He knew from past experience the futility of arguing with his brother. He started away from the porch.

Bo said quickly, "Where are you going?"

He answered without troubling to turn. "Back to town. I want no part of this."

Bo sucked in his breath. It was inconceivable that any Benton would refuse to side with his clan. "Hey, wait, you can't run out on us." He came down off the porch with a small rush, and Vance unwillingly faced him.

"I know what's the matter with you," Bo said. "It's that damned nurse. She's making a fool of you the same way that she's making a fool of Hy West. She's man hungry, and everyone in town knows it."

Vance hit him then. He struck once, his knuckles cracking into Bo's jaw, lifting the younger Benton clear of the ground and dumping him into a sitting position on the hard earth.

Vance did not even look at him again. He walked quickly to the corral, picking a rope from the fence and stepping inside to catch up a fresh horse. He saddled and mounted. Bo still sat where he had fallen, fingering his aching jaw. Vance rode away.

It was almost daylight before he re-entered Soda Springs and rode down the alley to the dark livery. He turned the horse into the corral, went inside and stretched out on the bedding in an empty stall. He lay on his back, staring up as the first morning light found the chinks between the warped siding. He did not sleep. He tried to think, but no matter how hard he puzzled he could not unwrap the twisted pattern of the future.

When it was full light he could remain quiet no longer. He rose, walked out to the rear trough, stripped off his shirt and plunged his head and shoulders into the chill water. Afterward, feeling refreshed, he started to use the comb which Wentworth kept on a shelf in the office. Then, hearing a rig, he stepped into the still shadowed entrance of the runway.

A buckboard was coming toward him along the street. He recognized it at once. Bo was driving and his mother made a small figure at Bo's side. He knew even before they passed him and entered the station yard that this was the start of his mother's trip to the prison, that Condon's scheme for releasing his brothers was already in motion.

Vance held his place until the train came in from the east and he saw his mother board it. Having no desire to meet his younger brother, he left the livery by the rear door and found a scanty breakfast in a Mexican restaurant. Later he sought the barber shop and was shaved.

And finally he went to the Apache Hotel and strode into the lobby.

Andy Lawrence stood behind the desk, and the boy looked up in surprise as Vance came in. Benton was not an ordinary visitor at the hotel.

"You want something?"

"To see Laura Hall."

Andy, along with half the town, had been watching the meetings between the Eastern girl and Benton with sharp interest. More than once Andy had considered relaying what he knew to Doctor West, but a reluctance which was almost entirely foreign to his nature kept him from talking.

Now, however, he hesitated. West had come in only a few minutes ago, the first time he had left the hospital since the morning when Gimble's mob had tried to load the patients onto the train.

There had been no more trouble. Omstead, with the help of the imported railway police, had patrolled the grounds night and day until the epidemic ran its course. The last patient had been sent out yesterday afternoon, the makeshift ward was empty, and West had turned the hospital back to Gruber.

Andy said, "I don't think she wants to see you." He said it resolutely, but not too certainly. He was a little afraid of Vance Benton.

Vance was in no humor to be put off by the boy. "Supposing you let her decide that, Bud."

Andy resented being called Bud, but there was a look in Vance's eye which he did not like. He slid from his perch on the high stool and started toward the dining room. Then he stopped. Hy West was coming down the stairs.

West looked at the boy, and then at

Vance, and the question in his eyes was plain. Obviously he had heard what had been said.

He came down slowly. He reached the bottom of the stairs and said in a low voice, "Go on out front, Andy."

More than anything else in the world, Andy would have liked to remain, but he knew Hy meant exactly what he said.

He passed Vance Benton and went out, letting the front door swing shut behind him. Left alone, the two men eyed each other in studied silence.

West finally broke it by saying, "I'd like to know why you want to see Laura."

Vance Benton was uneasy before West's steady gaze, and this feeling of uncertainty gave him a touch of quick anger.

"Does that mean you pick out the people Laura can talk to?"

West said evenly, "There's something here that I don't quite understand."

"What is there to understand?" They were fencing and they both knew it. It was very unlike Vance Benton to attack a subject indirectly.

"I didn't even know you knew her."

Vance's smile was paper thin. "There are a number of things you don't know, *Doctor.* While you've been nursing the plague life goes on. There's no reason not to tell you. I know her real well, maybe a lot better than you do."

West's own reaction puzzled him. Perhaps the emotional vacuum which so often follows surprise explained his seeming lack of feeling at the moment.

He started to say something and then changed his mind. "I'll get her," he said, and went into the dining room. Laura was at the kitchen table, eating a delayed breakfast. At sight of him she looked startled. She had not known he was through at the hospital.

"Why, Hy —"

"There's someone in the lobby to see you."

Surprise narrowed her eyes. "To see me?"

"Vance Benton."

For a moment she did not move, but color swept up into her rounded cheeks. West saw the color and understood at once that this relationship had gone very far indeed.

For her part, the girl was trying desperately to think of the proper thing to say. She had known, of course, that sooner or later she would be faced with a showdown of some kind, but she had not expected it to come so soon, certainly not this morning.

Vance had never dared come openly to the hotel before.

She gave up finally, letting her eyes fall away from West as she rose and went quickly out through the dining room. West's head twisted to watch her, and when he turned back he found Belle Callahan watching him.

She had been at the sink when he came in, and he had been too abstracted for the moment to realize that she was there.

"How long has this been going on?" he asked simply.

She answered without hesitation. "It isn't my affair, Hy."

"I'm sorry. I shouldn't have asked you. I'll ask her." He came over to the table and sank tiredly into a chair. She took one look at his face and then lifted a cup from the shelf. She filled it from the coffee pot and set it before him.

"It's been going on quite a while. I think everyone in town knows but you."

He closed his eyes. He was not a person who indulged in self-pity and he was not indulging in it now. He wasn't even thinking of himself.

"But why Vance Benton?" He sounded puzzled. He was puzzled.

"He's a man," Belle said. "That's about

184

all there is, I guess. A man and a woman. I don't pretend to like her, but I have seen her face after she's been with Vance. She looks like a different person."

"She might have told me."

Belle came over and sat down at the table. "I suspect she's been fighting it," she said. "I think she didn't want you to know because she hoped it would pass."

"She didn't want to burn her bridges. Is that it?"

Belle found no answer.

He let his breath out slowly. "You'd have to know Laura to understand how impossible this is. She's the original girl who wanted things. She had a hard time when she was young. She never told me how hard, but I probably guessed more than she realized. She had her life all figured out. That's why she refused to come back here with me in the first place. She wanted me to take a resident's job at the hospital. That meant security and a fair degree of comfort. How can she hope to have either with Vance Benton?"

Belle said slowly, "I don't think she does. I don't think she wants to marry him. I've watched her during these last few days. It's almost as if she were trying to escape from a trap — and yet she can't seem to stay away from him. It's hard on you, to find out this way since you loved her."

He looked at the girl sitting across the table from him, so utterly different from Laura, as different as night from daylight, big where Laura was small, calm where Laura was nervous, seeming content with her niche in the world, wanting independence enough to take this job at the hotel.

"Don't waste too much sympathy on me." He gave her a wry smile. "I suppose I loved her in a way. I suppose I still do. I was very young, and I knew nothing about women, and I was extremely lonesome and uncertain of myself. She taught me a lot. She helped me find a strength I didn't know I had, and I let her down by coming back here merely to prove to myself that I could make this town accept me on my own terms."

"You have," she said. "Even the ones who joined Gimble's mob are saying now that without you half the town might have died."

He said, "I've had no indication of it."

"And don't turn bitter, because you've lost your girl."

"I'm not bitter," he said, "and I don't accept the fact that I've lost her, as you put it. In a way I've won the battle that I came out here to fight. I hadn't realized it until

186

this moment. I no longer care what this town thinks of me. It's ceased to be important. I can look back at the people saved from the wreck, and the ones who had the pox, and know that I did a satisfactory job."

She showed her first unease. "Does that mean you're leaving here?"

"I don't know. I suppose Doctor Forbes would make a place for me if I went back. I had not intended to do it, but now that Laura has got herself involved perhaps it would be better. I think I owe her that much at least."

She was watching him, a faint frown growing between her brows. "Don't do it, Hy. Don't pattern your life to try and save her. You'll fail. You can't help her now."

He peered at her curiously. "You seem to know a lot about it."

"I do," she told him. "I'm a woman. Sometimes we don't reason like men. Sometimes we think only with our emotions."

"This from you, the girl who always said she wouldn't marry?"

She gave him a strange wry smile. "You may be a good doctor, Hy, but you still know very little about women." She rose and went back to the sink. He watched her in silence. . . .

In the lobby, Vance Benton was finding out that he too did not yet know all about women. Laura came quickly through the dining room, saying as she came,

"You had no business asking for me here this morning. What will Hy think?"

Vance had been alone with his troubled thoughts for most of the night, and his patience was near the breaking point. "What difference does it make what he thinks?" He tried to take the girl in his arms but she avoided him.

"Vance, stop it. Not here. Are you out of your mind?"

"Probably," he told her savagely. "Can you be ready to leave this town today?"

"Leave town?" She was thoroughly surprised. "What are you talking about? What's happened?"

"Never mind," he said. "We're leaving. I've made up my mind."

A trace of her old manner returned. "Now just a minute. You're going a little fast. I've never taken orders from anyone and I'm not about to start now."

"Look," he said. "I'll marry you if that's what you're worrying about."

"Oh, so now you'll kindly marry me."

"Goddam it!" He caught her shoulders, shaking her harder than he intended. "This is important. You don't think I'd let you go back to Hy West after what's happened between us?"

Under his touch some of her resolution crumbled. "Vance, stop, please. I can't think clearly when you're pawing me. What has happened? Don't you think that I have the right to know?"

He almost blurted out the whole story, but he was not completely certain of her full loyalty, and the code which had held him to his brothers was too strong.

"I'm in no trouble," he said harshly. "But I've split with my family. I'm getting out. There's no reason for me to stay in Soda Springs. I'll go anywhere you want to go so long as it's a long way from this town. Isn't that what you wanted?"

She didn't know what she wanted. She seemed to be a huge well of uncertainty. She could not make up her mind.

"Let me think."

"Think, then."

"Not now. I can't seem to think now. Give me a day or two. Give me a week. This is all so new, and so horribly important."

Black despair seemed to engulf Vance. A week. He did not know exactly what day the prison break was planned for, but he doubted if they would wait a week. And he had to be out of Soda Springs before the break; he had to if he wanted to stand clear of it and the events that would follow.

"To hell with it then." He let her go. Ignoring her protesting cry he slammed his way from the hotel. She stood straining after him, almost running after him. But at last she started toward the stairs. She had gone half way up when West's voice reached her.

"Laura."

She stopped, but did not look down at him.

"Hadn't we better have a talk?"

Her voice was listless, as if all emotion had been drained out of her. "What is there to talk about?"

He said with a tinge of irony, "I'd think there were several things. Won't you come down? I hardly care to stand here shouting."

She came back down the stairs like a sleepwalker who has no control over her legs. "All right. What is there to talk about?"

"Vance Benton. What was he doing here?"

"He came to ask me to marry him." She was rapidly recovering her old poise. The need to defend herself renewed her confidence.

"And you answered?"

She did not deny his right to know. "I

asked for a few days to think it over."

"Which means you're considering it?"

"Which means I'm considering it."

They stared at each other for a moment like two strangers. He said, "This is no good, Laura."

A trace of listlessness returned to her voice. "Nothing's very much good, Hy. I'm sorry, but sometimes people can't help the way they feel."

"They can't," he said. "But have you thought about the future?"

"It's all I've thought about." It was a cry, a word of desperation. "How can I marry him, Hy?"

"You can't." He said it bluntly. "Marriage is more than an emotional disturbance, more than the act of giving yourself to a man. It's a partnership. How can a person like you be partners with Vance Benton?"

Suddenly she was crying, softly, but as if her whole control had given way. "I can't get along without him, Hy. I can't. I never felt this way about anyone else, not even you. I'm not sure it's love. I guess I don't know what love is. I only know that when his hands are on me I can't refuse him anything."

He looked down at her bowed head. He

had never seen her like this before, humble and afraid.

"What's he want you to do?"

"To go away with him today. Something is pushing him, Hy. I don't know what, and he won't tell me. Could you find out? Would he talk to you? I think he's scared of something. He said he'd split with his family and there was no point in staying in Soda Springs. He said he didn't care where we went so long as he went a long way from here."

"And you told him?"

"That I had to have time to think. But thinking does no good. Nothing does any good."

"All right," he said. "I'll talk to him. In a way I got you into this. I guess it's my business to try to get you out."

chapter 16

The main building of the Territorial Prison dated back to early Spanish days. The place had been rebuilt and enlarged, but enough of the original structure remained to give it a marked resemblance to a medieval castle.

Abel Hunt owed his appointment as warden to the political ring which flourished in the capital, and he had paid his debt by filling most of the positions at his command with friends and relatives of his political associates.

The prison doctor was no exception. Dr. Mathews had learned what little medicine he knew by rolling pills in the office of a small Missouri town doctor, and had purchased his diploma from one of the diploma mills which flourished through the country in the Eighties.

But general practice had proved both hard and unremunerative and he gladly accepted this prison post which a brother-in-law had secured for him.

A nervous man, uncertain and apologetic before his equals, he could be vicious and cruel, and he was hated thoroughly by both the prisoners and guards. The prison itself held the prize collection of criminals which could be gathered from all over the Southwest, murderers and thieves whose names were by-words of robbery, of rape and of ruthless killing. But even in this select company the two Bentons had managed to build a small notoriety for themselves. As usual, they were confined in solitary when their mother arrived.

The doctor was in the warden's office when word came that Mrs. Benton wished to visit her sons. She was carrying a letter from Dr. Condon which explained that because of age and failing health it would probably be her last chance to talk to either of the prisoners.

The warden was a careless but not an unkind man, and both he and Mathews owed Condon favors from the past. He read the letter, shrugged, and gave his permission.

Ma Benton walked along the stone corridor to the visitor's room, looking small and tired and old. The prison building awed her as nothing else had ever done. It was so huge, so massive, so obviously strong, that she began to understand Condon's evident reluctance to undertake the break. Considering these stone walls, it did seem that no man could possibly hope to escape.

She sat waiting, and her iron composure almost cracked at her first glimpse of her sons. Both had aged, and their thin dark faces bore a certain pallor which is mostly associated with death. Nor was the pallor the only mark. Their eyes burned with a light which showed a hint of madness and made her almost fear them.

She waited until the guard had retreated to the door, and then she told them what was planned, repeating Condon's instructions minutely. Later she watched them being led away and offered up a silent prayer that the next time she saw them the boys would be free.

Afterward she left the grim old building and walked slowly to the railroad track, feeling weak-kneed and tireder than she had ever been in her life. It was with real relief that she saw Bo waiting for her beside the station in Soda Springs. She let him help her into the buckboard for the long ride to the ranch.

She saw the bruises on his face and asked how he'd gotten them. When he told her about his fight with Vance, she listened with her thin-lipped mouth tight as a steel trap. When he finished she said,

"Find Vance. Let me talk to him."

He left her beside the station, but although he searched the town he found no trace of his brother. It was Andy who told him that Vance had ridden out. Andy and Sam had watched from the station as the older Benton left the livery stable, but Andy did not know where Vance had gone. No one seemed to know. So finally Bo was forced to return to his mother with this information. He took her out of town at a high run, whipping the horses needlessly as a way of working off some of his suppressed anger.

Two days later Duke and Prince were reported sick. No one at the prison associated the fact with the visit from their mother.

The news reached Mathews while he was at breakfast. In the ordinary course of events he would have ignored it until he finished his meal. But such was his fear of the plague that when the guard reported the symptoms he hurried into the dark, lower tier which was commonly called the Hole.

Both Bentons lay on their bunks, and Prince was groaning softly, complaining of his aching head, the pains in his back and sickness at the stomach.

Mathews made certain that both had fever. He noted the redness along the hairline, and at once ordered them to the row of outbuildings which flanked the courtyard and had previously been used as stables. Then he wired Condon and sought the warden in his office.

"More pox."

The warden was short and fat and not inclined to worry unnecessarily. But he worried now. They waited for Condon to come; they got an answering wire instead. The lymph from the East had not yet arrived, but he was coming on the next train, bringing with him a Mexican who had had the pox and whom he had used to nurse some of the cases in town.

Mathews relaxed. He had an ignorant man's respect for Condon's knowledge and there was no reason why they should mistrust him or his Mexican companion.

Pedro was short and squat, and his face bore mute evidence of the pox's ravages. He moved with his bag of medicines into the empty stable next to the sick prisoners and from that moment took over their full care, bringing the food from the prison kitchen, and keeping the guards out of the improvised cells entirely.

Condon went back to Soda Springs on the evening train. He rode out to the Benton ranch long after dark to warn Bo that everything was working perfectly. He told Bo to gather his riders and be ready outside the prison at sundown on the fourth day. Then he returned to Soda Springs.

Andy carried the news that the doctor had been summoned to the prison when he came in for lunch, and he reported in the evening that Condon had returned. "I guess they've got the pox," Andy told West who was eating beside him in the long dining room. "At least he took a Mexican up with him as a nurse."

"How many cases?"

Andy was chagrined that he did not know. "I'll find out," he volunteered.

"Never mind," West said. "I'll talk to Condon tonight. Maybe it would be better if I went up there to help." He glanced across the table at Laura Hall. His first impulse was to suggest that she might accompany him to the prison, that there might well be sufficient work for a proper nurse.

Work would do her good. She had been like this for three days, ever since Vance had walked out of the hotel. She had not mentioned Vance's name. She was pleasant and reserved with everyone, but the spark had gone.

He glanced toward Belle. Belle had been wonderful these last few days, bestowing kindnesses on the other girl without appearing to. Belle had seen that Laura was kept as busy as possible during the daylight hours.

He rose and left the room, walking along the street. Several people spoke to him as he passed, people who a few short days ago would have pointedly ignored his presence.

He had won his place here, all right; won it with the help of the train wreck and the epidemic. And now that he had won it he did not care.

He felt at loose ends for the first time in years. There had been so little time for real thought since coming back to the Springs.

He wondered if the change in Laura was responsible for his inability to make up his mind about the future. It seemed very curious that they, whose lives had been so close, should suddenly find themselves little more than strangers.

But he knew deep within himself that Laura had nothing to do with his purposelessness. It went deeper than that. He was like an athlete who had practiced all his life for one event, and won it, and now saw no other purpose for his developed proficiency. His medicine had been a means to an end, a means of establishing himself in this town, of claiming what he thought of as his rightful place. And now that he claimed it the whole thing seemed empty and without real purpose.

I'm just tired, he thought. I'll take a few days until I get my feet under me, and then I'll go back to Chicago and see if Forbes will still give me the residence job. I may find enough to occupy myself in hard work.

He reached the fence before Condon's house. He peered over the fence, found the house dark, and thought, I should have known he'd be at Callahan's.

He turned away, just as Hamberger came from his shop and paused to lock the door. Then the saddler called across, "Looking for Condon?"

West nodded.

"He took his buggy out about two hours ago. I haven't seen him come back."

West thanked him and walked aimlessly along the street. He came to Callahan's, hesitated, then went in. The big room was nearly three-quarters full, men lined along the lip of the big bar, four poker games going at the rear tables.

He ordered a drink, the second since he had returned to town. He carried it to the rear, setting his shoulders against the old wall and watching the play of the cards at the corner table.

Behind the bar, Callahan had watched

him come in. He continued to watch without appearing to, studying West, analyzing him and somehow being dissatisfied with his thoughts. Two or three of the players turned their heads and nodded. It was a motley crowd: merchants from along Railroad Avenue, riders from the outlying hill ranches — and half a dozen soldiers from the fort who formed a hard knot at the front end of the bar, not mixing with the townsmen, taking their drinks in quiet silence, thinking of other pleasures which they might find later above the dance hall beyond the tracks.

Three times there were empty seats at one of the games and three times West almost sat in. He had no real desire for cards, but he was inwardly restless.

This was the town. Every shading of its social structure was represented within the room. If he were to remain here these were the men with whom he would be associated, and he thought with a detached bitterness that there was not a friend among them.

They were no longer hostile. They had accepted him on a kind of sufferance. Some of them even felt a little guilty at remembering that they had joined Gimble's mob in its attack on the station and the Railroad Hospital, but none of them made any real motion to include him in their circle.

Belle had been right, he thought. He had unconsciously held the world a little away from him. A man had to give something of himself before he had any real friends. Throughout his years in school, and his internship at the hospital, others had formed into small cliques, sharing their joys and their problems, while he stood almost alone. He had accepted this as his natural lot until Laura forcibly broke down his reserve. And then he had clung to her, holding fast to her in an effort to escape loneliness.

He knew now that he had never loved Laura. Always he had suspected her associations with other men, but time after time rejected the suspicion out of fear that it would break the relationship he had come to depend upon. And suddenly he realized that the severance of the relationship brought relief. Actually, his subconscious mind always had rebelled at the thought of binding his life to that of Laura.

But without her, what would he do? Would his work be enough? Could the hospital and its never-ending duties replace his desire for the tight companionship of a family which he had always wanted and never had?

His glass was empty. He walked to the bar

for a refill and found himself facing Callahan. He looked at the man curiously as the ex-sergeant set the bottle of whisky upon the bar. Callahan had made a success here, a far greater success than he had ever been able to contemplate while wearing a uniform. But he had traded much to achieve that success. He had lost his wife and now his daughter. He was alone with no one save a crowd of saloon loafers for companions.

He wondered, if Callahan had a chance to go back and live his life over again, what would his choice be? He was almost tempted to ask the man, and then, meeting the steady eyes, he held back the words. Callahan was a person he never could get close to. Callahan neither invited confidences nor returned them. Callahan had selected his road and plowed along it with all the determination of a headstrong bull.

West swallowed his drink, heard a rig in the street beyond the bat-wing doors, and walked the length of the room to peer out.

It was Condon. He saw the doctor travel the block and turn into his own drive and pull up at the barn.

West stepped out. It was nearly midnight and there were few loiterers. Bruce Gimble cruised down the far sidewalk, making his late rounds, and saw West and pointedly avoided him. West stood there for a moment, undecided, then moved up the street toward Condon's.

Condon came from the barn in response to the clamor set up by the dogs, and found West in the shadows. He felt a stab of quick fear, wondering if in some way the young doctor had learned of the planned prison break. Then his self-confidence came rushing back as he decided that this was impossible.

"Come in." His tone was ironic. "It's been a long time since we had the pleasure of your company here."

West did not speak as he followed the older man across the baked hardness of the yard and into the cluttered mussiness of the consulting room.

He took a chair, tilting it back against the wall, and watched as Condon cleared the table by the simple expedient of sweeping the litter to one end. Then without a word the older doctor produced two dirty glasses and set out a bottle from the desk's lower drawer. He watched while Condon poured a small drink into one glass and then half filled the other, raising it in a kind of silent salute before he downed the contents at a gulp.

"I've been expecting this visit."

"I've been rather busy." West's grin was mirthless. "I heard that they're having some trouble at the prison. I thought I might be of help."

Condon raised his eyebrows.

West felt his face redden slightly. It had always been thus between them, a gulf which for some reason neither could seem to bridge. Condon had the knack of making him feel that he was in the wrong, even when the older man did not apparently intend it that way.

"I'm through at the Railroad Hospital," he said. "There's hardly enough work for one man under ordinary circumstances, and I doubt if I'd stay even if Gruber were not here. It isn't what I want."

"What do you want?" Condon had poured new drinks without even asking West's desire.

"You asked me that once a long time ago," West said. "You were sarcastic then, and your question along with other things sent me away from here. I've never thanked you, either for that or for taking me in at the time of the trial."

There was an expression on Condon's face which West had never seen there before and which he did not understand. "I might have done more for you." The older man seemed to be talking to himself. "Perhaps I should have — and yet, I doubt that you would have come out as well. I'm rather proud of you."

West was startled at that. Despite everything that had happened he had never expected praise from Condon.

"Life's a funny thing." The older man was still speaking almost to himself. "We all make mistakes, stupid mistakes. But sometimes things turn out better than we have any right to expect." The whisky seemingly had loosened his tongue, but instead of sharpening its bitter edge as drink usually did, it mellowed him to a point that West had never before observed.

Then the tone changed, hardening a little. "Keep away from that prison, boy. They almost got you once, and it's better not to enter those walls. Besides, there's no real problem there, nothing for you to do."

He broke off to empty the bottle into his glass without offering any to West, and drank it at a gulp as if his throat were burning. Then, his speech noticeably thickened, he added, "Get out of Soda Springs. There's nothing here for you or for anyone else. I've found that out. It's a trap." The words died. He stared at his visitor apparently without seeing him. Then he laid his head upon his hands and slept.

West blew out the light and left the house. The street was entirely empty as he made his way back to the hotel. Lights still burned in Callahan's but there was no noise from the bar, only the steady clanking from the distant railroad shops and the chuff of a switch engine as it made up the eastbound freight.

He came into the lobby and was surprised to find Belle Callahan sewing under the light of the center lamp. He said, "Don't you work enough in the daytime?"

"It's Andy's shirt," she said, holding it up for his inspection. "Since Mary's been sick the kid is almost out of clothes." She looked at him intently. "Some coffee?"

He nodded and she led the way into the kitchen. Putting the pot on to boil, she asked, "Out celebrating?"

He grinned at her. "If you can call it that. I went down to ask Condon if I can help at the prison. He was out on a call so I visited your father's place."

She winced a little at that, and he leaned across the table impulsively, putting one hand over hers. "Can a doctor give you a bit of advice?"

Her expression was neutral, neither rejecting nor asking for his words, but he said quickly, "Your father's getting old, Belle. Don't cut yourself off from him too long. You might be sorry when it's too late. A family is a nice thing to have."

She did not argue. Instead she nodded slowly. "I'll think about it, Doctor. What about yourself?"

He said lightly, "Nothing about me. My only chance is marriage and that doesn't look promising at the moment. Not promising at all."

chapter 17

Andy Lawrence knew something was going to happen. He didn't know exactly how he knew it but he was as certain as if someone had told him. It was kind of like sensing that it was going to rain.

He'd had this feeling before, he confided in Sam Dillon. They were sitting on an empty baggage truck behind the express office and Sam's blue eyes squinted as he listened to Andy.

"It's this way," Andy told him. "It ain't just an idea I got. There's real trouble brewing. You just wait and see."

Sam did not argue. He was a year younger than Andy and he usually followed the older boy's lead. "You think the Bentons are up to something?"

Andy scratched his leg. "I just don't know. I figured maybe Vance and Doc West would start shooting each other over Laura, I did for a fact. But shucks, Doc acts like he don't even care."

"Maybe he's afraid of Vance."

"Shucks, he ain't afraid of nobody. Look

at the way he stood up all alone to Gimble and that mob. I'll bet you Vance Benton wouldn't have done that. You know something — I think maybe it's him being a doctor. I was talking to him and he was telling me about the oath a doctor has to take, something about saving life and such. Maybe doctors feel that it just ain't right for them to kill people."

Sam was thoughtful. "Come to think of it I never even saw Doc Condon wear a gun."

"He's got a shotgun," Andy said. They brooded on this in silence.

"What's Doc West going to do now?"

Andy hated to admit he didn't know. "He's just sitting around, doing nothing. I asked him was he going back to Chicago and he just grunted. I sure hope he does."

Sam was surprised. "I thought you liked him."

"Sure I like him, but if he was in Chicago maybe I could stay with him while I studied medicine." He glanced carelessly up the street and then stiffened. "Hey, there's Vance Benton riding in now. First time I've seen him in three or four days. I bet Laura will sure be tickled to see him. I heard Belle tell Ma she was plumb eating out her heart since he went away." He slid from his perch, followed by Sam, and together they started for the livery, a kind of unofficial welcoming committee.

Vance Benton did not see them coming. Vance's mind was busy with more important things. When he had ridden out of town he fully intended to keep on going until he was out of the country, and right now he was cursing himself for not following his first impulse.

But ten miles above the Benton ranch he had halted, then swung back, knowing that his mother would still be on her way to the prison, and that Bo probably would wait in town. Fred was away when he rode up, the ranch deserted. He packed food and coffee into a sack which he tied behind his saddle and then took the hill trail, winding onward until he found a vantage point on the flank of Mount David.

From this place he could watch the comings and goings of the hill ranchers. Often in the past he had amused himself by spying on his neighbors.

But this time there was more than amusement in his mind. For three days he watched, checking on both Fred and Bo as they rode in and out of the side canyons.

He guessed that they were alerting the men whom they had chosen to ride with them on the prison break, and the knowledge made him all the more uncertain and restless. For the first time in his life he seemed unable to make up his mind, and finally on the morning of the sixth day after his mother had gone to the prison he could stand it no longer.

He caught up the horse which he had kept hobbled in a little box canyon, and set out for Soda Springs, making a wide detour to avoid the possibility of meeting either of his brothers. He rode in, tired and dirty and unshaven in the shank of the afternoon. He left his horse in the corral and started along the alley, ignoring the two boys who watched him from the rear barn door.

He paid no attention to anyone, made no attempt to conceal his progress as he stalked along. He was a man with a purpose, and nothing would turn him aside from that purpose.

He reached the entrance to the hotel kitchen and came in without knocking, his arrival startling Belle Callahan so badly that she almost dropped a bowl of stewed apples. She managed to set it on the table, and then she scanned his unshaven face.

"What is it, Vance?"

"Laura. I've got to talk with her."

Belle did not argue. Without a word she left the kitchen, climbing the stairs to

212

knock on Laura's door.

"Who is it?"

"Belle. Vance is in the kitchen."

The door opened almost at once. Beyond the girl Belle had a view of the bed, an open letter and an unwrapped package. Laura's face was white, her eyes troubled and uncertain. "What shall I do?"

Belle was practical as always. "You'd better talk to him. He looks as if he's had a bad time."

"I can't. It's no use."

"Look." A hint of annoyance had crept into Belle's practical tone. "Go ahead and talk to him. If a man wanted me as much as Vance seems to want you I'd at least talk to him."

There were tears in Laura's eyes. "I'm afraid to. If I see him again I'll probably agree to anything he wants."

"Why not? I understand he's broken with his family. Let him take you away from here."

Laura gave her a thoughtful look, then went past her. Belle hesitated. It was time to start supper but she must stay away from the kitchen. She went into Laura's room and sat on the bed.

The package lay open and she saw a picture inside. She was about to shove it out of her way when she noticed that she had seen the picture before. She sat there several minutes before she remembered. Yes, of course. It was the tintype which for years had hung above Doctor Condon's desk.

She picked up the letter which lay beside the package and read:

My Dear Miss Hall:

The enclosed picture which you forwarded to Messrs. Gill and Brush of Arch Street is a likeness of my daughter Mary. This picture was given to her husband, Doctor Silas Jordan, at the time of their marriage. I am extremely anxious to know where you secured this picture as I have spent the last twenty years in a vain effort to trace Dr. Jordan.

When he and my daughter separated he took their two-year-old son with him and we have never heard from either since. Any information concerning the whereabouts of the doctor or of the boy will be very very welcome to an old man. My daughter died long ago and there is no one left but me.

Very respectfully,
Phillip DeLong

Belle Callahan read the letter twice. Condon must be the missing doctor, but the boy . . . ? Why should Laura have had the picture? Why did she send it East? Did Laura think that the missing child was Hy West?

She pored over the letter, her quick mind exploring the possibilities, the implications. If West were Condon's son, that would explain why the older doctor had taken the boy in at the time he was threatened with prison. But why had the boy been placed with the Bentons to raise? And why had Condon failed to tell the boy who he was, saddling him instead with the ridiculous name?

She had no answer. She walked impatiently into the hall. She wanted to talk to Laura. She wondered how soon it would be before the girl finished her conversation with Vance.

Half an hour passed before Laura came through the dining room into the lobby. Belle hurried downstairs to meet her, carrying the picture and the letter.

Laura was radiant, too excited to notice the letter in Belle's hands. "It's all settled." She was nearly crying. "Vance and I are going East on the midnight train. There's a man in Texas who will give Vance a job.

We'll be away from here and I can find out if I can stand ranch life."

Belle said, "That's wonderful," and meant it. She held up the letter. "I found this on your bed."

Laura was still too filled with her own affairs to pay much attention. "Yes, it came on the afternoon mail."

Belle hesitated. "Isn't the picture the one that used to be in Condon's office?"

Laura nodded. "One day I went out there to get some morphine —"

"You stole it?"

Laura flushed. "I don't know why. I haven't liked Condon ever since Hy told me how he was treated when he was a boy. And I had a hunch. I felt that Condon was hiding something. I didn't know what. So I took the picture and mailed it to the photographers."

Belle said slowly, "And you think Hy is Condon's son?"

"It could be. Why don't you have Hy ask Condon?"

"Why should I be the one to tell Hy?"

"Because you're in love with him."

Belle gasped. Laura took both her hands. "Belle, Belle, stop trying to fool yourself. I knew it when I first came. I resented you because I thought I wanted Hy myself. But

216

since I met Vance it's different. You're the only friend Hy ever had in this town. He used to talk about you, back in Chicago. I was jealous of you, even before I came."

Belle didn't answer.

"Show him the picture," Laura said. "Let him read the letter. He's all mixed up. You can straighten him out if anyone can."

She turned away, running upstairs to pack. Belle stared after her, then slowly went on through the dining room to the kitchen.

chapter 18

Ordinarily there was but a single guard in the prison courtyard, but as soon as the Bentons had been transferred to the old stables the warden put an extra man on duty.

All day, Prince and Duke had been too restless to lie on their bunks. Only the Mexican, made stoic by his Indian blood, waited patiently for the coming of darkness.

There was no way in which they could be certain that Fred and Bo would be posted in the arroyo with their men for the rendezvous at sundown. It was a chance they had to take.

The sun dropped slowly, the shadows lengthened across the yard, and the two guards stirred restlessly at their post. One was tall, the other short. Nondescript men, unimportant. The tall one was named Brem, the short one Curly Bill.

They stood together in the shadows and Joe Brem said, "I don't like it." He spoke too loudly as a weak man often does in an effort to reassure himself. "I never did care much for this job and with the pox it's worse. The head guard doesn't like me. He always gives me the dirty jobs."

Curly Bill spat on the worn stones. He was a rider out of the wasteland to the west, and only accident had put him here as a guard rather than an inmate. He was guilty of a hundred petty crimes.

"No danger us catching the pox as long as we stay in the air. My brother died of it. I was with him. We was prospecting the Gila country. I just kept away from him, and I didn't catch it."

"Then how'd the Bentons catch it? They were in solitary."

Curly Bill did not know the answer. He did not want to think about it.

Inside the old stables, Duke Benton sat fingering one of the guns which Pedro had smuggled in with his bag of medicine. Duke was a big man, the biggest of the five brothers, but no longer as strong as he had once been. Prison had softened his muscles and turned them flabby.

"Time yet?" His tone was irritated and impatient.

The Mexican moved to the tiny window and peered out. "Bo say half an hour after the darkness."

"It's that now. Let's get going."

Duke stood up. The Mexican nodded. He

slipped the gun under his belt, opened the door and vanished into the courtyard. Duke and Prince waited, the guns in their hands, ready.

Curly Bill saw Pedro emerge. This was standard procedure. The Mexican would cross a corner of the yard to the kitchen wing and return with the prisoner's supper.

But Pedro was getting closer to him than Joe Brem liked. The man would be carrying germs on his clothes.

"Get back, keep away from us," Brem called.

Pedro turned away, but as he turned the gun came from its hiding place below the belt. He fired twice, accurately, his bullets dropping them both. He ran in then, seizing Brem's rifle as Duke and Prince bolted from their doorway to join him.

There was a guard on the wall at the corner. He foolishly stepped into view, and Prince dropped him with a shot from Curly Bill's rifle. Then they raced for the heavy gate, tearing at the chain which fastened it, finally shooting away the massive lock.

Bo came yelling into the yard, leading an extra horse. Duke lifted himself into the saddle.

Prince never got to his horse. They did not know from which direction the bullet

220

came. It must have been fired from one of the windows of the main building. The whole place was in an uproar.

The outlaws now had control of the courtyard and the wall guard station, but of course they could not break into the main building. It never occurred to anyone within the massive structure that the men in the courtyard would try to get in. The prisoners were escaping. The only thought in anyone's mind was to stop them.

The warden himself opened the main door and led the rush of the guards into the courtyard. The warden was one of the first to die.

The guards who survived the first volley tried to retreat, to bar the door, but Bo Benton seemed to go crazy at their attack. He had been marshaling his men for withdrawal when the guards came out.

He swung, riding directly into them, clubbing about him with his heavy-barreled gun, blasting into the faces of the guards, taking a wild, savage joy in the battle and excitement. Eight guards were killed in the courtyard before Bo rode his horse into the main hallway. The doctor was almost the last to die. He died in the warden's office where Duke Benton had forced his way in search of the master keys. The doctor died without a fight, knocked from his chair by Duke's bullets.

The outlaws were in control of the main prison. The surviving guards had retreated into the stone tower which stood above the solitary cells and barred the door. The whole building was in tumult, excited prisoners clamoring for release, shrieking their curses as Duke passed them by.

Duke made his selection with care. He picked only men whom he had learned to respect within the walls. But after he had freed those he had chosen to accompany him, he flung the keys into the nearest cell, not caring whether or not they were used to release the rest.

He had freed eleven men, but there were not horses enough for them. It was necessary to raid the prison stables before they could be mounted.

As they dashed from the stables there was a red glow from the kitchen wing, and a minute later the windows burst, the flames shooting out to lick upward toward the sky. The whole action of the break had taken less than ten minutes.

Cateye Smith had been the leader within the prison walls. Cateye was one of the toughest killers the border country had ever produced, and he tried to assume leadership of the mounted men as if by natural right.

"Let's move." He reined in beside Duke Benton. "This place will be swarming with marshals by tomorrow."

He was interrupted by Fred Benton who pushed forward, leading a horse across which he had thrown Prince. "We've got to get a doctor," Fred said. "Prince is hit bad."

Duke grunted. He hadn't known that his brother was wounded. Cateye glanced briefly at the unconscious man. He said, "Leave him. We got no time to waste."

Bo had come up on the other side of Smith, still carrying his rifle. Bo still had the wild glaze of excitement in his eye. He did not know who Smith was and did not care.

"Shut up," he snarled. "I'm giving the orders here."

Smith looked at him, his light eyes muddy with anger in the growing glare from the burning prison. Bo held the rifle ready. The men from the hills swung behind Bo in a tight knot.

Smith was no fool. His chances of escape would be better if he held company with the Bentons and he knew it.

"What do you want to do?" he demanded.

It was Bo who answered. Bo in the emergency showing unexpected leadership. "Two of you ride over to the railroad and make sure the telegraph wires are cut. Fred, you head for Soda Springs and get Doc Condon. Bring him to the ranch if you have to drag him at the end of a rope."

Smith had no idea where the Benton ranch was. He was not familiar with this portion of the country. He said, "Is that heading toward the border?"

"Never mind the border," Bo told him. "We'll get Prince to the ranch and hide him back in the hills. Condon and Ma can look after him. Then we'll head for Mexico. Let's ride."

They rode, twenty-three men in all, heavily armed, the prisoners carrying weapons captured from the guards. Behind them they heard the shrieks of trapped men as the fire gained in volume until it seemed to fill the sky. Bo had Prince before him, on his horse, trying to hold his wounded brother upright, not knowing whether or not he would live until they reached the ranch.

At almost the same time Hy West came into the hotel kitchen, finding Belle there by herself. She turned and nodded, then went on frying the steaks for dinner. "There's something on the table you might be interested in seeing. Did you ever really wonder who you are, Hy?"

He looked at her curiously, pondering what prompted the question. "Of course. Anyone would, in my situation."

"Does it make a lot of difference?"

He sighed. "I guess so. At least it would have once. Now I'm not so sure." He walked over to the table, where the picture and letter lay enclosed by the loosened wrappings, and pulled them out. He recognized the tintype as the one which had hung in Condon's office and stared at it in puzzled surprise. He glanced toward Belle for explanation, but her back was turned. He picked up the folded letter, noting as he opened it that it was addressed to Laura Hall.

Belle continued to concentrate on the stove, so he read the letter, a frown deepening between his brows.

When he finished he said in an unnatural voice, "Where did you get this?"

"From Laura."

"And how did she happen to have it?"

Belle pushed the skillet back off the fire and came over to him. "Sit down," she said.

He had the picture in his hands. He sat down, poring over it, not lifting his eyes as she told him of Laura stealing the picture, of her mailing it to Philadelphia.

At last he said, "So you think this is a picture of my mother?"

"We both do."

"And I'm Condon's son?"

"It seems so. It makes a certain amount of sense that way. It would explain why he took you in instead of allowing them to send you to prison. All you have to do is to ask him."

He said slowly, "If he'd wanted me to know he'd have told me before this. What's to keep him from merely saying that the baby mentioned in this letter died? Maybe it did."

"Maybe."

"And I'm not too sure I want to claim Condon for a father. Perhaps I'd be happier not knowing who I am."

She said steadily, "You know what you told me about my father and myself."

"That's right."

"I know how you could find out without approaching Condon. Ride out and talk with Ma Benton. Tell her you know Condon is your father and see what she says."

He folded the letter thoughtfully. "Where's Laura?"

"Upstairs, packing. She and Vance Benton are leaving on the midnight train."

He showed no surprise. She watched him, recalling what Laura had said to her. She had always known that she was in love with him. Through all the years of his absence he had seldom been out of her thoughts. It came as a real shock when he returned, and a worse shock followed when Laura appeared. She had resolutely tried to put him out of her mind, and she had failed.

She yearned over him as he sat holding that picture. She wanted to reach out and comfort him. She wanted to take him into her arms and hold him close. She knew how he felt. It must be confusing, even upsetting, to discover that after all these years he might have living relatives, that this stranger who wrote from the East might be his grandfather, that Condon might be his father.

He rose, stuffing the picture and letter into his pocket. "All right, Belle. I'll talk to Ma."

"And then?"

He shrugged. "It will depend on what she tells me. And after she talks it will take some thinking." He started toward the dining room door, but stopped just before he reached it. "Say good-bye to Laura for me, and wish her luck. It's better that I don't see her, I think." He was gone then, leaving the hotel and walking up the street.

He had traveled less than half a block when Andy ran across from the station to fall into step. "Where are you going?"

He hesitated. There was no real reason why he should not tell the boy. "Out to the Benton ranch."

"Why?"

They had reached the corner of the livery stable. "I want to talk to Ma."

"What about?"

"Look," West said. "When you get to be a doctor, then will be the time to ask questions. A doctor is supposed to ask questions and find out all he can about his patients. But other people aren't. It's kind of impolite. Now, run on home. Belle was already cooking the steak when I left."

Andy hesitated, but could think of no way to refuse. He scuffed slowly back along the street as West went on to the corral after a horse.

Vance Benton watched West saddle, wondering why West was going out to the ranch. Twice Vance almost walked out to stop him, but he stayed hidden in one of the stalls. He could not be sure that the break was set for tonight, and if it was, his brothers would certainly head for the border and not go anywhere near the ranch.

After West rode away, Vance rose and brushed the straw from his clothes. He stepped into the dark livery office and checked the clock with the aid of a lighted match. It was seven o'clock, five hours until train time.

Vance was not a praying man, but he hoped with all his soul that nothing would happen in the next five hours, that he and the girl would be on the train, headed away from trouble.

He washed at the trough and ate in the railroad lunchroom. Then, as he had done on the night of the train wreck, he went into Callahan's and sat at the poker table. He was too nervous to enjoy the cards, but he wanted to be certain that if the break did come tonight a number of people could swear he had been thirty miles away in a poker game.

He played so intently that he did not see Condon come in and seat his bulk in his usual place, but the doctor stared at him so fixedly that he finally turned.

For Condon it was something of a shock to see Vance quietly playing cards while Bo and Fred were helping Duke and Prince to crash their way out of the prison. He had chosen to be seen in the saloon for the same reasons that Vance had joined the card game.

He waited with increasing nervousness for the flash to come, telling the town of the escape. The fact that Vance had held clear of the plot was troubling, since he had much more confidence in Vance's judgment than in that of the other boys. The game dragged on, a series of small pots, with no forging ahead of a real winner. At eleven Vance tossed in his few remaining chips and moved past Condon to the bar. He was standing there, having another drink, when the bat-wing doors swung open and Fred eased into the room.

Vance saw him in the back-bar mirror and stiffened. His brother spotted him, gestured guardedly and slipped back into the night. Apparently no one had noticed Fred's arrival — at least no one paid any attention.

Vance moved casually to the door, pushed it open and stepped outside, his heart thumping so loudly that it seemed everyone in the saloon should have heard it.

Fred leaned against the corner of the building, white-faced and exhausted. He told Vance what had happened in quick, terse, choppy words. He had almost killed his horse getting here. He could hardly stand.

"Send Condon out to the ranch," he said. "Send him quick."

Vance cursed under his breath. Less than an hour more and he would have been safely on the train. But Fred stopped that hope also. "We cut the wires," he said, "and pulled up three rails. That was Cateye Smith's idea. There won't be a train through for some hours."

A pall of depression settled over Vance. He still wanted no part of this. He thought of getting horses and taking Laura into the hills. But the city-bred girl would not be able to ride far and as soon as the news of the prison escape was broadcast the hills would be safe for no one.

"Go to Condon's," he told his brother. "I'll get the doctor there as soon as I can. And a couple of horses, too."

He drifted back toward the saloon entrance, savagely resentful. Why had Prince had to stop a bullet? Why hadn't they headed for the border as originally planned? The whole thing seemed a conspiracy to involve him. If he went into the saloon now and dragged Condon out, everyone in the room would later associate the act with the break.

And then he heard someone whistling and saw Andy leaving the railroad station and cutting across the street toward home.

He called softly and stepped out into the

center of the street to meet Andy. He slipped a dollar into the boy's hand.

"Look," he said, "Laura and I are leaving tonight."

Andy had already wormed the information out of Belle.

"I want to see Doc Condon before I go, but I don't want everyone in the saloon to know I'm leaving. Get Doc. Tell him someone's hurt and waiting for treatment at his place. Don't tell him it's me or he may not come."

The boy nodded and ducked toward the saloon door. Vance disappeared into the livery, caught up two horses and had saddles on them by the time Condon came along the street. He followed, not noticing that Andy also was following farther down the block.

Condon did not hear Vance. The doctor entered the yard, went up the path and pushed open the door. He saw Fred Benton and stopped. "What are you doing here?" he rasped.

Vance was almost at his heels, thankful that the dogs knew him and had not set up a clamor. He put a hand against Condon's back and pushed him into the room.

Condon swung on him savagely. "What's going on?"

Vance said tonelessly, "They broke into the prison as you planned. Prince stopped a bullet. He's at the ranch."

"At the ranch? What in the hell are the fools doing at the ranch?"

"They took Prince there. They had to take him somewhere, and they sent Fred in after you."

"Not after me," Condon's jaw set. "I'm all through. I've had enough. I warned them to get across the border as fast as they could ride. God damn it, the fools should know this country will be alive with men as soon as the news gets out."

Vance was in no mood to argue. "I've got horses saddled, Doc. You and Fred better ride while there's still time."

"No. I'm through."

Vance took a step toward him. "You aren't through, Doc. You're going."

For an instant Condon seemed to be measuring Vance Benton. Then a crafty light glowed in his eyes. "All right. I'll get my bag." He turned toward the desk as if to reach for the bag. Vance sensed what he was about, and before Condon brought the gun free of the drawer Vance shot twice. Both bullets struck Condon fully in the chest. The old doctor dropped his gun. He fell forward and lay still. Vance did not even give him a second glance. The dogs were howling outside. He opened the door to swear at them and as he did so he saw Andy Lawrence peering over the fence beside the gate.

Vance could move fast when he chose. He sprinted across the yard and through the gate almost before the boy could drop from his perch. Andy had no chance to run. Vance grabbed his arm and dragged him inside almost before Andy realized what had happened. But before Vance reached the house with his young captive the town behind him seemed to go crazy.

Vance stopped and listened. Whistles were shrilling in the roundhouse. Men were shouting. He heard the slap of several shots. Soda Springs had come to life with a bang.

He dragged the boy inside, answering Fred's question with a snarl. "I don't know what's happened. Get some rope and tie this kid up. Gag him if you have to. Then wait here. I've got to get word to the boys that Condon isn't coming, that they've got to get away from the ranch. If I don't show up here by daylight watch your chance and slip south. If they catch you you're as good as hung right now. But you're safe here. The dogs will keep people away. Just don't answer if anyone hails the house and keep the light off. They'll think Condon's away or drunk."

He slipped back through the rear gate to the alley and along it toward the livery stable. And now he realized fully what had happened. News of the prison break had reached the town. Nothing else could explain the feverish excitement. He did not know that the news had been wired to the West Coast, and then relayed back along the eastern line to Soda Springs.

The message had been so garbled in transmission that no one understood all of it. But the prison was still burning and a good many of the guards were dead. Most of the prisoners had escaped and many of them had scattered afoot over the rough country to the south and west. The track had been torn up and no trains could get through. This much was understood.

The first message had been received at the railroad station just as Vance stepped from the livery stable to follow Condon up the street, and the news spread across town, the sound of the whistles and the resulting excitement blanking out the noise of the two shots which killed Condon.

Vance did not dare to appear on the street, and he had no chance to ride away from the livery stable unobserved. Already the sheriff was forming his posse in front of the building and requisitioning horses for his men.

Vance crouched in one of the empty stalls, trusting to the darkness and the turmoil to conceal his presence, and from the stall he heard the sheriff conferring with Bruce Gimble and the major from the fort.

Messages poured in constantly, and the call boys ran them over from the station as soon as they were received. The situation was clearing somewhat. The deputy warden who had led the guards when they took refuge in the prison tower had sallied out and already he and his men had rounded up half a dozen of the lesser prisoners. The fire was still burning, and they wanted help at once.

The Territorial Governor called on every peace officer in the southern district to form all available men into posses and appealed to Washington for the use of troops. The War Department granted permission and Major Clayborn ordered out three companies, leaving only a few men at the fort.

Omstead made up a special with box cars for the horses, and the troops were loaded as fast as they rode into town. The rough plan was for the cavalry to be shipped the thirty miles to the prison. Using the prison as a base, Clayborn was expected to string out his men westward in an effort to close the border.

The sheriff and his volunteer posse were to ride northward into the breaks in a giant half-circle, hoping to drive the escaped prisoners between them and the screen of cavalry which Clayborn would fan out.

"The Bentons engineered this." It was the sheriff talking. "The word is that the fighting started when the Bentons broke out of the old stables where they were quarantined, and that they opened the gates to riders from the outside. And the Bentons know every foot of those northern hills."

"You don't think they'd be fools enough to go back to their ranch?" Bruce Gimble asked.

"I stopped guessing what the Bentons would do years ago," DeMember said. "If I was in their boots I'd head directly for the border and get across before Clayborn could spread his line. But we've got to cover as much ground as we can."

The major nodded. "The Department is sending a detachment from Yuma. I'll make contact and work back this way. They will cover to the west of the prison. A posse is working down from the capital and another from Sweetwater, directly north of the prison. If you can comb the breaks and then

237

pivot to meet my men, we ought to have them boxed in case they're still north of the line."

He turned as an aide brought word that the special train was loaded. "Good hunting," he said, and left for the station. Ten minutes later the posse rode out, almost a hundred men, leaving Soda Springs deserted save for women and a few railway workers.

As soon as he felt sure they had gone, Vance slipped back into the alley. The corral behind the livery was empty and the two horses he had so carefully saddled were gone. For an instant he stood staring at the bare enclosure. Then he thought of the horse in the doctor's barn. He ran back down the alley and threw a saddle onto the animal's back. He would have liked to say good-bye to Laura before he left town, but there was no time.

He swung out across the flat desert a good fifteen minutes after the posse, but he was not worried about reaching the ranch first. He knew the slanting mountain trails as he knew the lines of his hand. Without trouble he could cut a good ten miles off the route which DeMember's men would follow. The question was, could he get back out again, bringing his brothers with him?

chapter 19

Hy West had taken the main trail to the Benton ranch, and he came into the valley unchallenged. He stepped from his mount at the corral fence and crossed the yard toward the lighted house.

He did not realize that Ma was sitting on the shadowed porch until she rose and sent her query across the darkness.

"Who is it?" She had been waiting there since sunset, waiting for news from the prison, knowing that one of the hill boys who had ridden with her sons would circle back and bring her word on his way to his lonely ranch. Most of the men who had gone with Bo and Fred meant to come back. There would be nothing to link them directly with the prison break, and therefore no reason why they should accompany the Bentons to Mexico. But she had not expected West, and she did not identify him until he answered her hail.

She stood at the edge of the porch, trying to keep her voice steady, trying not to conceal the nervous anxiety burning inside her.

"What are you doing here? What do you want?"

He moved up into the path of light from the front window, saying quietly, "I want to talk to you, Ma. It's important."

To Ma Benton, nothing was important save news from the prison. She had been sitting alone, cursing the age which would not let her accompany her sons, an old woman, bound by a weakness she hated to admit.

"There's nothing for us to talk about, Hy West."

She had to get rid of him before the messenger arrived. She did not want him here when news of the break came. She did not trust him. In fact she would have trusted no one on this night.

"There is something," he said. "I've found out who I am. I want to ask you some questions."

She was surprised.

"I asked you a few weeks back," he said. "There's no real reason why you shouldn't tell me everything you know."

She bit her lip, trying to think quickly. "If I tell you, will you go? Now?"

For the first time he sensed her nervousness. He had thought it strange that she should be alone on the dark porch, that there were no horses in the corral, and he wondered suddenly what the Bentons were up to this night.

"What is it, Ma? Where are Bo and Fred?"

She said angrily, "That's none of your business. Did you come out here to spy?"

He felt sure now that something was wrong. He knew her too well not to recognize her uneasiness, but the last thing he wanted was to be mixed up in the Bentons' affairs.

"Why should I spy on you?" he said. "All I want to know is why Condon never admitted he was my father."

She was startled, then relieved. "Have you talked with him?"

"Not yet. I wanted to talk to you first."

She said slowly, "I don't know too much. He brought you here when you were just a baby. He paid us to raise you. He didn't explain anything then, but once or twice when he got drunk he talked. He'd gotten into some kind of bad trouble back East. A woman he operated on died, and his wife left him because of it, and he couldn't practice. I don't know the whole thing, but he admitted that he stole you from your mother and brought you out here. Your mother's father was hunting him and hunting you, and he was afraid that if they found a doctor with a little baby and no wife they might trace him down. Besides, he couldn't take care of you himself."

"I can see that. But why didn't he tell me later? Why didn't he tell me at the time of the trial, when he took me to live with him?"

She hesitated. "You're asking too many questions — some you'd be better off not to have answered. He hated your mother for not standing by him when he was in trouble, and he was drinking a lot. He told me once that Condon wasn't his real name, and that there was no use giving it to you. I think he loved you, Kid, in his own way. But he was also afraid that if you knew, you'd ask questions about your mother, about his former life. Questions he didn't want to answer. He isn't much of a man."

West didn't comment. They sat there silent in the darkness, and suddenly there came the whispered sound of many horses coming up the trail. The old woman stiffened with a gusty little cry.

The number of horses scared her. There should be only one messenger, two at most. What had happened? Was this a posse already coming, looking for her sons?

West was on his feet, staring down across the dark yard. "What is it, Ma?"

She did not answer. She stood speechless,

one bony hand clutched to her thin old breast.

And then they burst into the valley and were at the corral fence. He could not judge their exact number, but they made a black knot beyond the row of poles. Duke and Bo came toward the porch supporting a sagging form between them, and Ma ran forward with a sharp moan. They brushed by West, carrying Prince, still dressed in his prison garb.

Inside, they stretched Prince on the old couch. West, who had followed to the doorway, saw that the man's face already bore the grayish pallor of death.

Bo turned and saw West. "Hy? Good. You're a doctor. Have a look."

No questions as to how he came to be there, nothing in their excitement save the knowledge that he was a doctor. He stepped forward to bend over Prince.

The bullet had gone in below the shoulder, and almost certainly it had nicked a lung. He was surprised that the man on the couch still lived.

He heard them talking around him, heard them telling their mother about the prison break.

He bent over Prince again. He had not seen this man since the last day of the trial, and Prince had once been his boyhood hero.

Strange, he thought, how your sense of values changes. He no longer identified himself in his own mind with these foster brothers.

He was cutting away the bloody shirt, and asking for hot water, and Bo was at his elbow, no longer hostile for the moment, asking how much chance Prince had.

He wanted to say, none. The bullet hole was a little higher than he had at first supposed. Perhaps it had missed the lung at that. But the shoulder was shattered and the bullet had lodged just under the shoulder blade.

"I haven't my instruments," he was not speaking to Bo; he was thinking aloud. Prince should be dead. Only a man with the vitality the Bentons had could have survived so long.

"Condon's coming," Bo said. "He'll have some tools with him."

"He'll never come." It was Duke's bitter voice. "The old Doc thinks too much of his precious hide to venture into these hills tonight."

"He'll come," Bo said. "He'll come because he does think a lot of his precious hide. He knows that if he doesn't come I'll make certain that he hangs for Dave Lawrence's murder."

West had been sponging the blood from the broken shoulder. He stopped. "Say that again," he told Bo.

"You mean about Dave Lawrence's murder?"

"That's right."

"Condon shot him in the back. I saw him do it. Dave was on to the fact that Condon had been planning our holdups."

West turned back to the wounded man. Ma was standing across the couch, her thin hands clasped across her breasts. For an instant their eyes met, and in that instant West saw something in her face that he had never seen there before: compassion for him.

He went on, bandaging the shoulder now, and when he looked up Ma's shriveled lips formed a question: "Will he die?"

West shrugged. He did not know. He finished the dressing and stepped out onto the porch. Nothing further could be done until Condon got there. He wondered exactly how he would react when he met his father. He thought bitterly, The one man I really respected here was Dave Lawrence, and my father has to be his murderer.

He looked out across the dark yard. He

knew now why Ma had said there were questions about Condon which were better left unanswered.

Bo came out onto the porch, followed by Duke. Together they moved down to where the escaped men had built a fire, close to the corral. West trailed them, not because he was interested in the former prisoners, but because he felt that he had to get away from the house.

Cateye Smith had risen from his place beside the fire and came forward to meet the Bentons.

"How is he?"

"Bad," Bo said.

"We've got to move." Smith glanced behind him toward the canyon's bottleneck. "If they catch us in here we're dead."

Bo's voice tightened. "We can't move until the doctor gets here."

The men around the fire heard him, and a grumble ran through the group. West listened to the argument with only half an ear, for he had caught the sound of a single horse, coming fast up the canyon. He stood still, analyzing his own reactions, wondering what he would say to Condon, what he could say to Condon, and then the fugitives heard the oncoming rider and were springing to their feet, catching up their guns.

But the rider who came into the circle of firelight was not Condon. It was Vance Benton.

Vance pushed his horse directly at Bo and swung down. His younger brother gave a grunt of surprise.

"Where'd you come from?"

"Soda Springs. I saw Fred. There's hell to pay."

"Where's Condon?"

"Dead."

A tremor ran through Hy West. He turned away, hearing Vance say behind him, "He wouldn't come. He tried to pull a gun on me."

West thought, I suppose I should hate Vance. I suppose . . .

But somehow he did not hate Vance. About his father he felt only a quick relief. Condon was dead. It closed the book as far as he was concerned.

Vance was talking rapidly. "The whole Territory is up. The troops are out, and DeMember is leading the biggest posse I ever saw to keep you from crossing the border."

They were silent, staring at him. Vance's anger turned on Bo. "I should leave you all to rot. It was bad enough making the break. It was a fool's choice coming back here."

Bo said sullenly, "I suppose you'd have left Prince to die."

"We'll probably all die now. How is he?"

"Bad. West is here, but he hasn't got his tools. He says he'll have to operate. We were counting on Condon's medicine bag."

Smith walked back to the fire. Men gathered around him, ready to pull out. Vance glanced back at them. "How many men can you count on?"

"Four. The rest of the hill boys have taken off for home."

Vance was thinking. He said softly, "I've got an idea. Soda Springs is drained of men. There aren't more than half a dozen left in town. We could ride in there and Hy could operate in his hospital."

"Smith and the rest wouldn't go." Bo sounded disgusted. "They're hell bent to get across the border."

"So much the better. Let them go. They'll take the main trail out of here and they'll run headfirst into DeMember and that posse. We can slip around to the east and take the shortcut for town. DeMember and Smith's men are going to fight the damnedest battle you ever saw. That should keep them all occupied while we get away."

Bo sounded dissatisfied. "And when we get to the Springs we'll be in a worse trap than we are here. The border south of there will be lousy with soldiers."

A devil had started to dance in Vance's dark eyes. "We've got a chance," he said. "That's all we can ask for — a chance. Remember when Gimble seized the railroad station during the plague? Remember how he pushed Omstead into making up a special to send the pox victims out of town? We can do the same thing. We can load our horses into a boxcar, and have the train take us fifty miles east. We can leave it in the desert, unload the horses and ride for the border. It won't be guarded that far away."

Bo and Duke were catching his spirit. Bo said softly, "It might work. If we told Smith he'd bring his men with us."

"To hell with them." Vance's voice was rough. "We need them to keep DeMember and the posse busy. When they run into the sheriff they'll scatter like quail. DeMember will spend the next couple of days trying to hunt them out of these hills. I'm going to talk to Smith. Just keep your mouths shut."

He went to the fire. Hy West followed, wanting to hear what Vance was going to say. Cateye Smith said hoarsely, "Well, what do we do now?"

"We're going to take my brother into Soda Springs," Vance said.

"The hell we are!" Smith took a step toward him. "We've wasted too much time already. If we'd headed out for the border first we'd be almost across the line by now." He vented his anger on Bo. "To hell with you Bentons. We're riding out."

Vance said, "Do you know the country?"

"We'll find our way. To hell with you."

Vance looked at him for a moment, then swung on his heel, catching Bo's arm and half dragging his younger brother away. Out of earshot of the mounting men he said, "They'll take the main trail until they get clear of the hills. They'll have to or get lost. Once on the plain they'll cut westward — if they get out of the hills before they run into DeMember's posse. I'm betting they won't make it."

Bo did not answer. Vance said, "Dig out those four hill boys and see if they'll ride with us." He motioned to West. "What chance have we to get Prince to town?"

"None."

"We've got to try it."

"Yes," West agreed. "You've got to try it." He trailed Vance into the house. Vance had taken charge. Bo and Duke were following his lead. West tried to analyze his feeling toward Vance and failed.

None of the events of this night had any sense of reality. He felt as though he were living through a nightmare. Condon was his father. Condon was a murderer. Vance had killed Condon. And of all the Bentons he had liked Vance the best.

And there was Laura to think of. Laura and Vance. What would happen to them now?

He heard Vance speaking calmly to his mother, telling her not to worry, that he would get them safe across the border, that she could join them later in Mexico. He wondered how much of this Vance actually believed. Vance was no fool. He knew how badly the odds were stacked against him.

Then they were in the saddle, with Prince in a crude litter between two horses, following the curving way down through the canyon mouth, cutting off on the hill path which would swing them eastward of the main trail around the rough, rugged face of Bald Mountain.

They rode as stealthily as Apaches — three active Bentons, four hill riders, himself and the unconscious Prince. All of them had grown up in this harsh country, all of them had followed this trail a hundred times. They knew each break, each rock, each twisted bend.

It was not until they mounted the shoulder and dropped over it that the whisper of distant rifle fire reached them from the west.

Vance, who was in the lead, halted them and they sat in their saddles, listening. It was too far away to tell exactly at what point the posse had run into Cateye Smith and his escaping prisoners. As nearly as West could judge it came from the western slope of Bald Mountain, which would put the battle a good twenty miles from Soda Springs. He had no doubt that Vance was right. As soon as they were attacked, Smith's followers would scatter back through the rough country behind the Benton ranch. It would take the posse hours, perhaps days to dig them out and run them down. Certainly there would be time for the Bentons to reach the Springs and perhaps escape eastward.

chapter 20

The sun was half an hour high before they came into the railroad town, but around them people were already stirring. Vance had given his orders well. He moved directly on the station and the roundhouse, seizing the night operator before the man had a chance to flash the news up the line that the outlaws were upon him.

They got Omstead in his bed, and Grantline before the dispatcher had time to dress. They herded the night crew out of the roundhouse, the switchmen from the yards, and marched them over and locked them in Callahan's.

It was done neatly, rapidly and almost silently. Within five minutes they were in complete control of the town. The few able-bodied men who had not ridden out with the posse showed no inclination to fight the Bentons.

They even seemed anxious to help the outlaws in their escape, prompted to this course by their desire to get them out of town as quickly as possible.

West knew very little of these activities. Prince Benton had been carried directly to the Railroad Hospital, and West sent Bo to the hotel for both Laura and Belle.

Surprisingly, Prince was still alive, but West doubted that even with his amazing vitality the man could survive the operation.

Bo came back with the two girls and stood gazing down at his unconscious brother while West made ready to operate.

"Think he'll make it?"

West shrugged.

"Can we take him with us?"

"He'll die for certain if you do."

"Even if we took you along to watch over him?"

West had not considered that. He had been giving very little thought to himself. He looked at Bo levelly. "It wouldn't make any difference. The shock of the operation will probably kill him. I'd say that he has one chance in a thousand, but the bullet has to come out. However, if you're going to insist on taking him with you there's no use to operate. He'll die anyhow."

Bo said savagely, "He'd rather be dead than go back to prison. Go ahead, start cutting." He turned and went through the door.

West scrutinized the two girls. Neither

254

had spoken since entering the room. Laura's eyes were swollen. She had been crying. Her hands trembled as she placed the instruments to sterilize. He had never seen her this way before and he said sharply,

"Steady, Hall."

She flinched. "What's going to happen, Hy?"

"I don't know."

"It's my fault." The blonde girl said it in a monotone. "Vance wanted me to leave with him earlier. If I'd gone he wouldn't be involved in this."

West shook his head. He guessed that he had never really understood Laura. A prison had been burned, fifty to a hundred desperate men were in the hills trying to escape, the whole Territory was up in arms, the town had been taken over by the Bentons — and her only thought seemed to be that, because of her, Vance remained here in danger.

There was nothing he could say, and it was obvious that in her present condition he could put little dependence on her help.

He glanced at Belle. She was composed, as steady as always, but she too looked as if she had had little or no sleep, and his tone was sharper than he intended when he asked,

"What's the matter with you?"

"It's Andy." She said it in a low voice. "He didn't come home last night. We spent most of the time looking for him."

He started. "But where —"

"We don't know. He was at the station just before eleven. The operator said he started home. Then, my father says, he came into the saloon after Condon, and told them there was an accident case at Condon's. He and Doc went out together."

A wave of cold fear washed over West. "Did you go to Condon's?"

She nodded. "But Condon wasn't there. No lights, and the dogs wouldn't let us into the yard. We went around back and looked in the barn. Condon's horse was gone."

West seemed lost in speculation so she said, "The only thing we could think of was that Andy had gone along with Condon. You know how he is. He likes to get his nose into everything."

"I know." West found that his own hands were trembling as he turned back to the table. He did not tell her that Vance Benton had killed Condon. He was afraid now that Andy had witnessed the killing, and that they had done away with the boy.

A sudden rage at the Bentons went up through him. His feeling for Andy was something of which he had not been quite conscious. Andy was a reflection of the debt he owed Dave Lawrence. The boy had no father, even as he'd had no father. He had so much in common with the boy.

But it went deeper than that. Andy with his inquisitiveness, his alertness and his boundless energy, was likable for himself. He had been the first to greet West on West's return, and he had made it very plain that he thought the young doctor was wonderful.

All those things — and now perhaps Andy was dead.

He focused his attention on Prince Benton's wound. He began to work. Prince died before the ether could take effect. West was neither surprised nor shocked. Among the hundred operations in which he had assisted at the hospital, there had been an average percentage of deaths. Death was something a doctor had to accept as his eternal opponent.

He rolled down his sleeves slowly, saying in an undertone, "You can tell Vance that he doesn't need to worry about Prince any more." He looked at Laura, then went into his own office.

Belle Callahan followed him. Belle was in the doorway when he pulled open the drawer of his desk and lifted out Dave Lawrence's guns. He turned after fastening the cartridge belt and saw her watching him with big, frightened eyes. It came to him as a shock that he had never seen her frightened before.

She said, "What are you going to do?"

"I have an errand, Belle. Go back to the hotel."

"You won't try to stop them?"

"We'll see," he said, and left by the side door. Actually, he did not know exactly what he meant to do. First, he wanted to visit Condon's house. He found it almost impossible to think of Condon as his father. The term included so many things that had little or nothing to do with blood relationship. He knew now that he would always remember Condon, not as his father, but as a crusty, untidy figure who had little love for his fellows.

He stepped into the center of the street, looking up and down its length. It was startling to see it so near deserted at this hour of the day. The citizens who still remained in Soda Springs were conscientiously keeping well out of sight.

One of the hill riders stood guard at the door of Callahan's, holding the captives inside. Another was planted directly opposite the station, where his rifle could control the full length of the street.

The other two and the Bentons were in the yards, overseeing the making up of the special train. West walked up the street toward Condon's, wondering if the men would challenge him. But he had ridden in from the hills with them, and they had known him as a boy, and they merely nodded as he appeared, apparently assuming that he was on an errand for the Bentons.

He passed the livery stable and moved on down to Condon's house, taking the precaution of drawing one of his guns before he pushed open the heavy gate.

The dogs came at him in a rush, one of them springing toward his throat. He waited until the exact instant, and then knocked it down with a sweeping motion of the gun barrel.

The dog lay for an instant stunned, then struggled to its feet, running toward the rear of the house, yipping as it went. Its companions had fallen back, watching him narrowly, their teeth bared, their ruffs high.

He seemed to ignore them as he went up the path. One of them dashed in to nip at his heel. He swung quickly and his lifted boot sent the wicked animal half across the yard.

The rest drew away, their coyote blood making them cautious. West reached the door and paused for an instant, steeling himself for what he might find inside. Then he pushed the door open.

Condon lay where he had fallen, but Fred had thrown a blanket over the body. West stared at the lumpy shape and then saw the boy bound on the couch at the side.

He crossed the room, seeing Andy's eyes widen above the top of the handkerchief stretched across the small face to hold the gag in place.

West freed Andy, gathering the slight body tight in his arms, holding him close. A reaction such as he had never known set in, and he was trembling as he finally set the boy on a chair and dropped to his knees, before him, rubbing circulation back into the small cramped legs.

"You all right?"

Andy's tone was not quite as self-assured as usual. "Sure." He tried to smile. "It wasn't so bad as long as Fred was here, but he left when he heard the horses on the street and I didn't much like being alone with him." He indicated the blanket-covered figure with a slight gesture of his head.

"I can imagine."

"Vance shot him."

"I know," West said. "Let's get out of here. Your mother and Belle are worried about you. They've been hunting you all night. Come on, if you can walk."

Andy could walk. He complained of needles in his legs and held firmly to West's arm, but after the first hobbling steps walking came easier.

The dogs snarled at them from a distance but made no real effort to attack. They crossed the yard, using the rear gate rather than the front, and moved along the alley toward the Apache Hotel. Now that Andy was safe, West had no intention of trying to stop the Bentons. He shared the feeling of the rest of the town. The sooner they were out of Soda Springs the better for everyone.

No matter what happened now, they would have a rough time below the border, and any punishment they deserved would in a sense be satisfied.

He and Andy came into the kitchen, the boy beginning to yell as soon as he was inside the door: "Ma, oh Ma! I'm home!"

They heard a thumping from the right. They approached the door of the small store room. It was fastened on the outside, so West pulled the bolt and pushed the door open.

Mary Lawrence almost fell out into his

arms. "Thank God you're here." She was nearly beside herself. "They've got Belle."

He steadied her to a chair, knowing that she had not yet completely recovered from her operation.

"Who's got Belle? What is all this?"

"The Bentons. They came to the hotel to get Laura's things. The fool is going with them."

"Who came?"

"Vance and Bo. They got her things and came downstairs, and then Bo grabbed Belle and told her she was going too." The woman stopped to catch her breath. "Belle tried to fight him off and I tried to help. Vance pushed me into the store room and bolted the door —"

West was already running out through the dining room. As he crossed the lobby and burst onto the gallery he saw the special train, already made up and standing beside the station platform. It consisted of a switch engine, a freight car into which the Bentons had loaded their horses, and an old coach.

He leaped into the street. The two riders who had been left as guards were heading toward the station. Vance Benton's special was about ready to pull out.

He ran harder. He saw Duke standing beside the engine, a gun in his hand, flanked by one of the hill riders. He saw Vance and Fred at the coach steps, motioning for the guards to hurry, and then he saw Vance turn and mount the car. There was no sign of Bo. The youngest Benton probably was in the coach, standing guard over Belle.

He shouted. He had to stop them before the train began to move. If he failed, there was no telling how long it would take him to catch up with them — and he knew with a flash of insight that if the Bentons succeeded in getting out of town with Belle Callahan, he would never stop until he tracked them down.

He didn't run toward the coach. He ran toward the engine. The engine was the key. Without it they could not move the train. He ran, shouting, and then he threw a bullet at Duke who stood covering the engineer. He missed. He heard the spang as the lead slug crashed against the side of the boiler.

Duke had been caught entirely by surprise. Even before he recognized the running man, he snapped off a shot. It kicked up dust beneath West's feet. The rider beside Duke was firing also, and Fred Benton and the two hill men from the street were shooting at him from an angle. It seemed impossible that all of them could miss him.

And then he had unexpected re-enforcements, for at the sound of the first shots the men imprisoned in Callahan's ventured to the door, and finding their guard gone, boiled out into the street.

The fireman and engineer took a hand. The fireman came down out of the cab as soon as Duke turned his back. He felled the hill rider with one blow of his scoop, and then charged at Duke. Duke whirled just in time to avoid the swinging shovel, and put two bullets into the fireman's chest.

But he did not escape for longer than a second. The engineer leaped from the steps, his burly form crashing into the oldest Benton and crushing him downward to the worn planks of the platform.

Seeing this, West changed his direction and ran diagonally across the station yard toward the old coach. He might well have waited for the re-enforcements from Callahan's, but it never entered his mind. His one thought was that Belle was on that train and he had to get her off.

Behind him somewhere, he heard Andy's squeaking yell, but he had no time to wonder what the boy was up to.

He stopped halfway across the yard, because his running shots had been far from accurate. He fired once, deliberately, and saw Fred Benton throw up both arms, spin and fall to the platform. He saw the hill riders duck under the car and start off across the yards.

And then Bo Benton came leaping down the coach steps. He fired at Bo. His bullet pinged off the coupling of the coach. He saw Bo raise his gun and fire, and felt the smashing shock of the bullet as it tore through his upper left arm.

He stood for an instant, steadying himself, wondering if he could hold his feet. And then he aimed and squeezed with desperate concentration. Bo Benton bent double, crumpled and lay unmoving on the sun-baked platform.

Hy West walked on, slowly, cautiously, his useless left arm hanging at his side like a broken wing.

And then he realized that Vance Benton was on the train platform, a gun in his hand. Vance was descending the steps haltingly, like a man approaching a chore which he disliked.

There was none of the frenzy about Vance which had marked Bo's movement. His eyes went over West's head, measuring the men who had broken out of Callahan's, but he had personally disarmed them before leaving them in the saloon, and he saw no guns in their hands.

It was West he had to worry about, and on West he centered his full attention. The game was already lost. He sensed this although he had not seen the action beside the locomotive. He sensed it before he stepped down to the planks and heard West's call.

"Drop it, Vance. It's all over."

Vance Benton made no motion to obey. He took a half step away from the side of the train. His gun hung loosely in his hand and for an instant it seemed doubtful if he would try to lift it.

"You've raised hell, haven't you, Kid?" There was no real anger in his tone, merely an acceptance of what had happened and what might yet happen.

West stopped and braced himself. Some twenty-five feet separated him from Vance. He held his gun a little higher than Vance but he did not aim it.

"It's over," he repeated. "Let your gun drop, Vance, and step away from it."

"Sorry," Vance said and sounded as if he meant it. "We're going through with this. There's no choice."

West didn't know whether Vance felt that there was still a chance to escape, or whether he thought his murder of Condon left him with no way out. And Vance gave him no time to decide.

Vance's gun started to swing up. West squeezed the trigger, thumbed back the hammer and squeezed again. Both bullets caught Vance in the chest. He staggered once, swayed, and then collapsed across Bo's still body.

West took no chances. He knew that Vance would have killed him if he could, would still kill him if he lived. He stood there watching, and he saw Laura Hall come down the car steps in a little rush and drop to her knees beside Vance.

And then the men who had been imprisoned in Callahan's reached him, and Omstead threw an arm about his shoulders, not seeing his wounded arm.

It was Callahan who reached his daughter first. Callahan came up behind Omstead just in time to see Belle appear on the car platform.

He rushed forward with a growl, and she came down the steps into his arms, and she told him what had happened. He listened, his face growing redder by the second. He had been inside the saloon and had not known that she was on the train.

He released her and grabbed West's hand. "You're all right, Doc. I won't forget it. I won't, and you can count on that."

It was Belle who saw West's arm, and his white face. It was Belle who made them take him into the hospital, and found Gruber, and stood over Gruber while he set the bone and bound up the arm. There were other patients by this time. Duke had been brought in, more bruised than hurt. Fred was still alive with a bullet in his hip and a second in his side. One of the hill riders had a hole in his chest.

They had hardly been patched up when the first wounded from the posse's fight with Cateye Smith's men began to come in. DeMember's men had hit them hard. Smith was dead, his followers scattered through the hills, and the sheriff was hunting them down, aided by riders from the capital.

The wire which the Bentons had cut on both sides of the station had been repaired. Reports flooded in. More than half of the escaped prisoners had been recaptured and the circle of troops and possemen was gradually closing in on those still at large.

Belle brought West the news late that afternoon, and Andy came with her to add his version. It was Andy who told him that Laura Hall had had Vance's body loaded into a wagon and hired a man to drive her out to the ranch.

"She sent word to you," the boy told

West. "She said to tell you that she didn't blame you. She said she guessed it had to work out this way, but she don't want to see you. She said she was going to take Ma Benton back East if the old woman would go with her."

Both Belle and West showed their surprise. Andy went on importantly. "And they've already taken Duke to jail. He wasn't hurt bad. Fred is going to die. That's what Gruber thinks."

"The end of the Bentons." Belle said it softly.

"It sure is." Andy was too active to stay long in the sick room, especially while the whole town was still buzzing with excitement and news kept drifting back from the posse hour by hour.

After he had gone Belle said, "I was sorry to learn about Condon. Did you get a chance to talk to Ma Benton? Was he your father?"

West nodded. He didn't tell her that Condon had killed Dave Lawrence. It would serve no good purpose for her to know.

"Don't feel too bad," he said. "The fact that we were related doesn't seem to mean very much."

"You can write to Philadelphia," she said.

"You can probably find out more about him in that way."

West didn't answer. At the moment he didn't want to think about Condon. His arm was aching and he was very tired.

"Speaking of fathers," Belle went on, "I made up with mine. He even offered to buy the Apache for me. Mary Lawrence is in no shape to run it."

He said, "Are you going to buy it?"

She hesitated. "I don't quite know."

He reached out with his good hand. "Belle, I've got something to say to you. I don't know what I'm going to do, whether I'll stay here or go back East. With Condon dead the town needs a doctor, and I might undo a little harm that he did from time to time."

"That's not a good reason for staying."

He said, "I've got another. You're here."

"Please, Hy, not now. I —"

"Listen," he said. "You once told me that you'd never marry a man unless he wanted you as deeply as Vance wanted Laura. Well, I found out one thing about myself today. That's the way I want you. As soon as I heard you were on that train, I knew. I knew that I'd follow you to the ends of the earth if necessary. I was going to let them go, without a protest from me, but when I heard about you —"

She kept her eyes down.

"I should have known sooner," he said. "I think the real reason I came back here was to prove to you that I amounted to something."

"That's what Laura said." The words slipped out before she realized she was speaking.

His hand tightened. "What did she say?"

Belle's face was stained with color. "She said I was in love with you. She said if I wanted you I should go after you."

He stared at her. "If you're thinking about Laura and me —"

"I'm not," she said, and dropped to her knees beside the bed. "I'm not." She kissed him then, and his good arm tightened around her.

Afterward he said, "We'll stay here. We'll help Andy study medicine if he still wants to, and doesn't decide to be a railroad man instead."

She didn't answer. She was content to kneel beside the bed, content to let her cheek rest against his, content to let their future take care of itself.

We hope you have enjoyed this Large Print book. Other Thorndike, Wheeler or Chivers Press Large Print books are available at your library or directly from the publishers.

For more information about current and upcoming titles, please call or write, without obligation, to:

Publisher
Thorndike Press
295 Kennedy Memorial Drive
Waterville, ME   04901
Tel. (800) 223-1244

Or visit our Web site at:
www.gale.com/thorndike
www.gale.com/wheeler

OR

Chivers Large Print
published by BBC Audiobooks Ltd
St James House, The Square
Lower Bristol Road
Bath BA2 3SB
England
Tel. +44(0) 800 136919
email: bbcaudiobooks@bbc.co.uk
www.bbcaudiobooks.co.uk

All our Large Print titles are designed for easy reading, and all our books are made to last.